Now the famous
Harlequin
romance
by Anne Mather
comes to life
on the movie screen

starring

KEIR DULLEA · SUSAN PENHALIGON

Leopard in the Snow

Guest Stars
KENNETH MORE · BILLIE WHITELAW

featuring GORDON THOMSON as MICHAEL
and **JEREMY KEMP** as **BOLT**

Produced by JOHN QUESTED and CHRIS HARROP
Screenplay by ANNE MATHER and JILL HYEM
Directed by GERRY O'HARA

An Anglo-Canadian Co-Production

WELCOME
TO THE WONDERFUL WORLD
OF *Harlequin Romances*

Interesting, informative and entertaining,
each Harlequin Romance portrays an appealing
and original love story. With a varied array
of settings, we may lure you on an African safari,
to a quaint Welsh village, or an exotic riviera
location – anywhere and everywhere that adventurous
men and women fall in love.

As publishers of Harlequin Romances we're
extremely proud of our books. Since 1949,
Harlequin Enterprises has built its publishing
reputation on the solid base of quality and
originality. Our stories are the most popular
paperback romances sold in North America; every
month, eight new titles are released and sold at
nearly every book-selling store in Canada and the
United States.

A free catalogue listing all available Harlequin Romances
can be yours by writing to the

HARLEQUIN READER SERVICE,
(In the U.S.) M.P.O. Box 707, Niagara Falls, N.Y. 14302
(In Canada) Stratford, Ontario, Canada N5A 6W4

or use order coupon at back of books.

We sincerely hope you enjoy reading
this Harlequin Romance.

Yours truly,

THE PUBLISHERS
   Harlequin Romances

The Gift of Love

by

MARGARET CHAPMAN

Harlequin Books

TORONTO • LONDON • NEW YORK • AMSTERDAM • SYDNEY

Original hardcover edition published in 1977
by Mills & Boon Limited

ISBN 0-373-02125-9

Harlequin edition published December 1977

CHAPTER ONE

A FLUSH of excitement spread over Francesca's thin face and she grew tense as she picked up the morning paper and once again read the advertisement which had caught her eye: 'Housekeeper wanted for composer living in remote part of Northumberland. Position suitable for mature, country-loving woman. Apply to Adam Greco, Old Beams, Kirklaw, Northumberland. Or telephone Kirklaw 303.'

Francesca's head went hot and tears pricked at her eyes. It was unbelievable! The famous composer and concert pianist at Old Beams! Famous, handsome, a debonair man of the world—she had often seen his picture in the papers. What could a man like that possibly be doing at such a place? And the Sutherland family had gone. Painful memories rushed back to destroy Francesca. Desperately she slotted another sheet of paper into her typewriter. She had worked for the solicitors, Paul and Charles Ducal, for over two years and had sent in her letters neatly and promptly for signature. This morning Mr Ducal was having to wait; Francesca's mind was not on her work.

'Mr Paul's waiting,' the office-boy told her impatiently. 'He has a meeting at eleven, Miss Lamb. He wants his letters.'

'Don't stand over me,' Francesca said with an unusual sharpness, and she reached for yet another fresh sheet of paper. 'Go on. I'll take them in.'

'Aren't you well?' The boy's face was pale with concern. 'I could tell him.'

'Go away. He doesn't often have to wait. There's no need to panic.'

'There's his bell again.'

Francesca paid no attention. She was far away from the musty old office, from the parchment and deed-boxes, from the solicitors whose faces were as chill and as humourless as their dingy office. She was back in Northumberland. She saw only the wild, undulating fells, she heard only the stillness of the moorland, she could smell only its sweetness. She saw only the long shadows cast by the trees on a bright, autumn morning and the wide frothy tide of sheep coming down from a plum-coloured sea of heather to the still, lush grass below in the valley. And suddenly, inexplicably, she could no longer bear London. She stood up and to the amazement of all around grabbed her coat and bag and without a word to anyone she left the offices of Paul and Charles Ducal for ever. She had made up her mind.

Five minutes later Francesca did not lie to the man who answered her call, for after her experience she felt most mature. And she was most definitely a country-loving person. The deep, richly masculine voice was honest too. There had been no other applicant for the position, Adam Greco told Francesca. He would be very glad if she would take the job.

Francesca left the telephone booth feeling happier and more alive than she had done for a long time. She hurried back to her flat, her shining brown hair swinging, her thin face flushed with excitement, her lavender blue eyes brighter and rounder than ever, the dimple showing at one corner of her sensitive mouth because she could not stop smiling. She had acted impulsively, perhaps foolishly, but there was no stopping her now. She was going back. Adam Greco had warned her of the isolation, but there had been no need for him to do that. She knew all about Old Beams. She knew every step of land for miles surrounding the old house. She knew Kirklaw as she knew herself. Yet, for some reason, she had kept this knowledge to herself. The past was dead, she would not have anyone stir it up.

Two days later Francesca was on her way north, back to the house to which she had at one time decided she could never return. But, of late, she had grown calm and a strange yearning had plucked at her heart. Her mother was dead, but her spirit still hovered over the land she had loved so well, and that spirit was drawing Francesca home. She had known for some time that she had to return to the little valley, to the grey stone cottage where they had lived so happily. To Old Beams where her mother had worked so hard as a housekeeper for so many years.

Turning grave eyes to the window as the train thundered north, Francesca thought for the first time of Giles Sutherland. She could think of him now without the violent revolt, the physical pain of battered pride; she was no longer rooted in self-pity. She could think of Giles objectively now. He had gone off to New Zealand with the girl for whom he had jilted her. They would be rich and happy. It was almost amazing to think that at one time she had been engaged to Giles.

Francesca's mouth tightened and for a moment she closed her eyes as though to blank out some pain. If only her mother had not been so let down. If only her mother had not gone off, overjoyed, to tell all her friends in the village how well her daughter had done. How foolish she had been, how human. It had made it all hurt so much. Her mother had been so kind, so understanding when the blow had fallen; when the Sutherlands had found someone more suitable for Giles ... a girl with wealthy parents and in their own social class. A rush of resentment and some of the old bitterness coloured Francesca's still face as she stared out at the flat land which spun by. If she suffered at all now, it was on her mother's account. She wondered if she had ever really loved Giles Sutherland. Perhaps she had merely loved the idea of him giving her mother a lift home in his car now and again to save her walking over the wet fields, for Giles had been kind.

Francesca had never thought of her mother and herself as being poor. They had been happy. For years her mother, widowed early, had earned enough money working at the 'big house' to keep them warm and snug in their small cottage, and during her childhood Francesca had imagined that the whole wide world had belonged to them. Now she was on her way, rushing back to her mother's beloved valley; to the wide-open fells, the heather-clad hills, to the little trout burn and the funny drovers' bridge which crossed it. She could almost hear the call of the moorland birds.

Francesca smiled sleepily and then changing her position thought of her new employer, Adam Greco. She had got the job because no one else had applied for it. He had told her that in an impassive, businesslike voice. But she had liked his voice all the same; it had a depth and richness which she could still recall. From all accounts Adam Greco had a following of rich, beautiful women and she had often seen pictures of the famous composer escorting one of them. Someone had written of him 'Debonair man of the world, brilliant musician. Watch out for this man.' Well, there should be no need for her to watch out for Adam Greco, Francesca decided. Brilliant musicians weren't interested in their housekeepers. And Adam Greco would never know that she, Francesca Lamb, had once almost become the mistress of Old Beams ... the wife of Giles Sutherland.

Exhausted now, Francesca slept, and when she awoke she was startled to find that the train was pulling in to the Central Station in Newcastle. She scrambled up and breathlessly thanked the man who helped her with her case, then hurried along the platform. Within five minutes she had found a taxi to take her up town to the bus station and ten minutes after that she had boarded the bus which was to take her to the Border hills and Kirklaw.

One hour later Francesca stood alone at a lonely cross-roads. Where was the person Adam Greco had sent to meet her? Five minutes later she was still standing there. Then, with a deep sigh, she picked up her case and started along the country road that headed west towards the moors and the great Wanny crags, the forest and the house Old Beams. She couldn't just stand there, she told herself, getting worked up and for some reason just a little nervous.

Francesca knew every inch of the country road; her gaze skimmed over the hedgerow as she walked. Each grass, each autumn leaf she knew by name, and now those names came back to her with a haunting sweetness. Then the road began to drop to the forest and the great bowl of land which she had called the Goose's Nest loomed up on her left. She paused for a moment to follow the peaty little burn which ran through the nest and then she began to make her way slowly up the hill.

9

The smack of hoofs on the road brought her to a standstill and she stood back on the grass verge waiting for a rider to appear. To her astonishment a pony and trap came down the bank at a rather alarming rate.

'Whoa!' the man holding the rein called. 'Whoa!'

The trap came to a standstill and Francesca found herself staring into a pair of magnificent dark eyes, the straight dark brows of which were lowered questioningly.

'Who the devil are you?'

The straight brows rose and Francesca thought she had never seen anyone with such glossy, dark, luxuriously waving hair—or indeed, any man so handsome. She stared in embarrassment at the owner of the trap, taking in his good features; his straight nose, dark skin, solid chin, sensual mouth.

'I don't believe it! You can't be.' Again the dark brows of the stranger rose.

'I'm Francesca Lamb,' Francesca said swiftly. 'I'm the new housekeeper ... I've been waiting at the crossroads.'

'Have you indeed! Perhaps I should apologise for keeping you waiting five minutes.' The dark eyes glittered and his mouth curved a little. 'I'm Adam Greco ... and I can see at a glance that I've made one colossal mistake.'

'Why?' Francesca asked, and stood back out of the way of the pony. 'Is there something wrong with me?'

His dark eyes skimmed over her as she waited for his reply.

'I wouldn't say that,' he said impassively. 'But I was led to believe that I had employed a homely, middle-aged woman.'

'Mr Greco, I didn't deceive you. I am both mature

and country-loving, as I stated.' Francesca met his gaze steadily.

'Good!' Adam Greco suddenly sprang down on to the road and with a smile took Francesca's case. 'Then if you die of boredom or the sheer isolation of the place I need suffer no pangs of conscience.'

'I don't intend to be bored, Mr Greco,' Francesca said quietly as she climbed up on to the bar seat of the trap. 'I love the country. I'm only half alive in the town.'

'For a city girl, you surprise me.' Adam Greco climbed up beside her and took the rein. He smiled as with a gesture he set the pony into motion. 'But then that's what makes life so sweet ... the surprises. The harmony and the discord, the bitter ... and the sweet.'

Conscious of his closeness, of the hard firmness of his hip against her own, Francesca moved away a little shyly, but found to her embarrassment that there was little room and that she could not escape either his hard body or the clean tangy smell of his skin. 'I expected someone a little older,' she told him, wondering at the same time why she sounded so aggressive and ill at ease. 'Someone at least forty.'

'Does that disappoint you?'

'No, of course not. Why should it? I merely said I had expected someone older.'

'Well, it seems that we've both got over our shock, so we'll push on, Miss Lamb. I hope you're not averse to riding in a trap. I enjoy the fresh air, so I often use it.'

For a few moments they drove in silence listening only to the smack of the pony's hoofs and the country noises all about them. Then Adam Greco asked, 'How old are you, Miss Lamb?' He gave her a swift smile. 'I

11

wouldn't be so ungallant as to ask, if I imagined you to be over twenty.'

'I'm twenty,' Francesca told him in a small voice, for she was now thinking of the small cottage which nestled in the valley just beyond the trees. In her mind's eye she saw Thorneyburn Cottage, her mother, the dog they had both loved and called Badger. With a surge of emotion everything came back and all colour faded from her face.

'I did tell you how isolated the place was,' Adam Greco said, glancing at Francesca and noticing her sudden pallor. 'But don't panic, I'm not exactly alone. I have a Mr and Mrs Noble living quite near by. Mrs Noble helps in the house and Thomas does a bit of gardening. I'm working hard at the moment, Miss Lamb, and for that reason I want as few people as possible around. I want silence ... and peace. You must understand that. I can't possibly have you asking all your friends out to Old Beams.'

'I do understand, Mr Greco,' Francesca told him in a faraway tone. 'And I have few friends.'

'You have parents?'

Francesca shook her head, but this time she could not answer him.

Again they drove in silence, this time starting along a rutted track which ran over the fields and up to the fells, across the old railway track, disused now, and on to the country lane that ran on to the old house which stood in the shelter of the forest and the crags behind.

'So you consider yourself to be a mature person?' Adam Greco remarked as they drove steadily along the lane. 'You've no doubt had much experience in life?'

'I have,' Francesca told him, frowning, and in a clipped voice, 'You don't need to worry about me.'

'I don't intend to worry about you, Miss Lamb. I've employed you not as a hazard but to be of some assistance.'

'Of course!' Francesca moistened her lips, reminding herself once again that she must remember her place. She was not driving back to Old Beams as mistress, but as a housekeeper. She straightened her back and took a deep breath, conscious of his scrutiny. In her mind's eye she could see him. She saw his dark, handsome face, the magnificent eyes which she guessed could fill with liquid fire or dismal melancholy. His mouth was strong and beautiful, the upper lip perfectly indented, the under one both sensitive and sensuous. He seemed polite, yet distant. But most of all it was his voice that attracted her; it was deep and rich, masculine, yet sweet, full of his own music.

'Do you know this part of the country at all?' he asked with an impatience she was sure he did not intend.

'My mother knew it,' Francesca answered truthfully. 'She used to talk about the North Country and the hills a lot. I know, for instance, that those crags must be the Wanny Crags. I also remember her talking about the old railway track.'

'The track that will never come back. There's a song about it now,' Adam Greco told her as they turned in through the large iron gates. 'But when the trains did run, they stopped at the bottom of my garden. Apparently one of the previous owners of Old Beams had a halt made for that very purpose.'

This time Francesca made no comment; once again her thoughts were far away, for now she could just make out the roof of Thorneyburn Cottage glinting in the twilight. It looked so silent and so still that her eyes

13

suddenly filled with tears, tears which she could not wipe away without giving herself away, so she just allowed them to run silently down her cold cheeks.

'You're very silent,' Adam Greco said as they started up the drive to the house and as the white pony kicked out at the drifting autumn leaves. 'Please don't be afraid.'

Francesca was not afraid, she was only sad. She stared at the dark, crouching rhododendron bushes which she could remember as a blaze of colour, and at the dark verges of earth where once she had seen a flood of daffodils. Some of the trees were almost stripped of leaves. It was almost winter.

Then she saw the house. It was just the same, a low brooding house with mullioned windows and a strong oak door. Behind it was an army of pine trees as invincible as nature herself.

'Here we are,' Adam Greco said as he jumped down and then held out his hand to assist Francesca. 'You see I was not exaggerating when I told you the place was isolated.' He picked up her case at once and strode off towards the door. 'If you'll go in,' he called, setting the case down just inside the hall, 'I'll see to White Cloud.'

'White Cloud?'

'My pony.'

'Oh!' Francesca smiled at the patient animal and gently stroked its neck. 'What a lovely name.'

'A present from a farmer's wife,' he called again.

'Haven't you a car?' Francesca asked as she picked up her case.

'Leave that,' he said and made a gesture with his hand. 'I'll take it up. Of course I've got a car—I'd do badly without one out here. Mr Noble has it this afternoon, though. He hasn't got one.'

Francesca stepped into the house she knew so well

14

and for a moment she stood as though spellbound. The old place had not changed, it was just as though she had stepped into the hall as she had done when she was ten years old to wait for her mother. The atmosphere was the same, the smell was the same, even the sounds were familiar. The square hall was just as dark as it had always been. In the dim twilight she could barely pick out the furniture, but she knew that the same old pieces were there and in their same old places. Adam Greco must have bought the house lock, stock and barrel. Grave-eyed now, Francesca moved from room to room, all of which led off from the hall. Finally she stood very still in the window of the dining-room, staring down over the undulating fields. She could just make out the seven ancient old trees almost bent to the earth by the west wind and which her mother had christened, affectionately, the seven old crones because of their bent, twisted old backs. Yet nature was kind, Francesca thought soberly. In spring she flung garlands of blossom over the old trees and in autumn she hung their grey fences with garlands of bright berries. With a sigh, Francesca wished for a little of nature's sympathy, a gay cloak to hide her own despondency. She raised herself on to her toes and pressing her face against the window she was just able to see the light which shone warmly from the windows of Thorneyburn House, which stood on a high ridge of rock further up the valley. She had heard her mother speak of the people at that house and she wondered now if they were still there. Then she heard Adam Greco's footsteps on the gravel outside and she hurried from the room, glancing in the sitting room door as she quickly made her way to the kitchen. The sitting room was just the same too, except that Adam Greco obviously used the room for his music study. A baby grand piano stood in the centre of the room and the alcoves were cluttered with recording equipment, records and tapes. There was a desk too, one she had not seen before. It stood in the window.

'Oh, there you are!' Adam Greco came stamping into the hall. 'Well, Miss Lamb,' he said, smiling charmingly and smoothing the deep wave of hair from his brow. 'Welcome to Old Beams.'

Francesca found herself breathing in deeply. For the first time she realised that Adam Greco was not very old, no more than thirty-two or three. In repose, she had already noticed that his features could wear an almost melancholy mask and he seemed older. She returned his smile and said, 'I may as well begin my duties straight away, Mr Greco. Do you usually have dinner in the evening?'

Adam Greco's dark brows rose and there was a gleam of mischief in his brilliant eyes. 'I hope you're not going to spoil me,' he said in a lowered tone. 'Up to the present we've been more or less helping ourselves, although Mrs Noble has made me a meal occasionally.'

'Occasionally? Then you must be starving.' Francesca gave him another quick, shy smile. 'I must make you something at once. In future, Mr Greco, you must at least have one good meal a day. I imagine you work very hard.'

'It would be pleasant if we could have a meal in the evening,' he said, studying her earnest face with a puzzled kind of humour touching his lips. 'But tonight, Miss Lamb, you are under no obligation. You don't start your employment in this house until the morning. I suggest you have something yourself and then take it easy. You've had a long day already, I'm sure.' He turned to go, then he glanced back and raising his eyebrows again suggested, 'Perhaps we could have a meal together each evening? Would that suit you, Miss Lamb?'

'That would hardly be the thing,' Francesca returned as swiftly as though she had just received a nudge from her dead mother.

'Perhaps, then, I could offer you a drink?' Adam Greco had turned his face to the shadows and she could not see his expression. 'Or what about some tea?'

'That would be nice,' she said as she took off her jacket and hung it up on the hallstand. 'But I'll see to it, Mr Greco. I'm sure you must want to get on with your work.'

'You seem to know your way around, Miss Lamb.'

His bantering words brought Francesca to a sudden halt. Her breath caught in her throat; she turned to stare at him and she felt the colour rise from her throat. She forced a little laugh and told him, 'I'm afraid most women know by instinct in which direction the kitchen lies.'

He frowned now. 'You're not one of these women's libbers, are you? I must say you don't look like a housekeeper. In fact, Miss Lamb, you almost embarrass me.'

'I've been many things,' Francesca told him quietly, regaining her composure. 'But I see nothing wrong in doing housework. I've been a typist for some time, and believe me, I'm glad to get back to household duties.' She shrugged her shoulders and told him as she turned to go, 'I suppose some people would call me old-fashioned.'

Adam Greco's brows nipped down now. 'I still don't fancy the idea of anyone so young turning into a hermit,' he told her with an air of genuine concern. 'There's very little for a girl your age to do here. Mrs

Noble is a nice woman, but I could hardly say she was your contemporary.' He seemed to smile at a sudden thought, then he added, 'There's Celia, of course. Yes, I must introduce you to my friend's wife. She's devastating and about your age.'

'I rather enjoy my own company,' Francesca returned, and for some reason she felt just a little put out. 'You don't need to introduce me to anyone, Mr Greco ... least of all your devastating friend.'

'No, no!' He raised a shapely hand. 'My friend is by no means devastating. But you'll see, his wife is quite stunning.'

Francesca went quickly to the kitchen and to her embarrassment she found that Adam Greco had followed her. He stood leaning elegantly against the doorpost as he watched her set the kettle on the Aga stove.

'All mod cons,' he told her. 'Deep freeze. Large pantry. Dishwasher, mixers and a cupboard crammed with provisions in case of snow.'

Francesca stood very still, staring about the kitchen she remembered so well. The Sutherlands had obviously sold their home with everything in it. There was the wonderful natural pine dresser which she had found so exciting in her childhood. The table and chairs were just the same and in their usual places. The walls had been painted and the floor newly tiled in a bright mosaic of colour, but it was the same room. Francesca turned away to swallow painfully. In this room, she reminded herself, her mother had spent most of her life.

'Is there something missing?' Adam Greco advanced into the room, his brows down again as he studied the slim girl who had come to be his housekeeper.

'Of course not. It's a very nice kitchen,' Francesca

said chokingly and turning away quickly to get down some cups and saucers. 'Any woman would love it.'

'I'm glad to hear it, Miss Lamb. But come to think of it I wouldn't like any woman in my kitchen.'

'You took a chance employing me.' She gave him another shy smile.

'Yes,' he said, considering her for a few strained moments. 'Perhaps I did, but I took a liking to your voice.' He straightened up. 'Miss Lamb, I must tell you at once that the Nobles live in a cottage. We're going to be alone, you and I, in this big old house.' He smiled slowly at the expression on Francesca's face, for it was truly at variance with the soft beauty of her body. 'I trust,' he said with a more gentle light in his own eyes now, 'that this prospect will not seem too daunting.'

'I expect to work hard and sleep well,' Francesca told him without flicking an eyelid. 'I won't get in your way, Mr Greco.' All the same, it was with an unsteady hand that she poured out the tea, and the look she gave him when inquiring, 'Sugar, Mr Greco?' was much too challenging.

He nodded and took the cup and saucer from her. 'You must give me time to adjust,' he told her, and a bright light came into his dark eyes. 'I'm sure you're going to be amazingly efficient.'

Francesca was not listening. She had moved away and now she was running a professional eye over the work units and drainer. She moved on to the dresser and stood for a moment, lost in thought, staring at it. Absently she pulled open a drawer and for a moment of sheer panic she thought she would faint. Her mother's old recipe book! It was still there just as it had been for all those years. Emotion filled her eyes with tears, the room swam. But she gripped the dresser hard, bit down her underlip until the pain was so bad that she could think of nothing else.

'Is there something wrong?' Adam Greco reached Francesca's side. 'You've turned deathly pale!' Concern sobered his face and made him even more darkly handsome. 'You'd better sit down, Miss Lamb. I'll open the window.'

Francesca sat down, lowering her head a little so that he could not see her eyes and the pain that was in them. Her thin face was stiff with emotion. Once again she saw her mother by the dresser, standing there examining her little recipe book. She could hear her saying, 'I must write this one down, Francesca. It's mighty fine. Don't you ever lose my recipe book.'

'Miss Lamb!'

Adam Greco's voice made her start and look up. Unsmiling, he had a noble face, a solid yet handsome face. She had never seen such wonderful eyes; so dark, like jet but streaked with lights of polished mahogany. 'I'm all right now,' she told him in a small voice. 'It's very warm in this room.'

'I'm afraid Mrs Noble doesn't believe in opening windows,' he told her, and for a moment he looked tight-lipped and severe. He studied Francesca for a sober moment. 'Perhaps it's something else that's upsetting you, Miss Lamb,' he went on sharply again. 'Perhaps you've already had second thoughts about taking this position. If that's so, then I'm quite willing to drive you back to Newcastle. I wouldn't like you to be frightened; either of the place or myself.'

'I like the house,' Francesca whispered. 'Why should I be frightened of you, Mr Greco? Have you a guilty conscience?' He gave her a hard look and, standing up, she went on quickly, 'Actually, I was thinking about something quite different, Mr Greco. The room is too warm and I must open the window more frequently. As for wanting to leave, that would be ridiculous. You've engaged a housekeeper, Mr Greco, and I have no intention of flying away.'

'Good!' He gave her a puzzled look, and then turned to go. 'That's settled, then.' Raising his hand in a gesture of finality, he strode from the room.

Alone, Francesca gazed around the kitchen as memories came crowding back. She went to the dresser and again opened the drawer. Tears crept to her eyes as she stared down at the worn, pathetic little notebook. She lifted her hand as though to reach for it, but she could not and with a fresh rush of painful memory she shut the drawer quickly again.

Walking over to the window, she stood stiff with emotion, her throat working, her lips trembling. Then she noticed the garden and she grew calm again. She remembered the garden so well. Sober-eyed, she stared out over the leaf-strewn lawns to where the yew trees still crouched like dark beasts against the old grey stone wall. The verges were dark now, but in spring they would be flooded with colour. She had grown up with those primroses, daffodils, hollyhocks and daisies. Beyond the wall the straight, tall pines still rose in homage to some deity they alone could see. Then the beauty of it all went swiftly from her mind, and her brow puckered up as she remembered how the Sutherland family had made such fools of both her and her mother. She thought of Giles Sutherland—and pitied him now for his blindness. As with his parents, money had been his god, a god to which he had been quite prepared to sacrifice her. Francesca sighed and turned back into the room. Now they were all far away ... her mother was dead; Giles and his rich wife were in New Zealand.

'Good evening!'

Francesca spun round, her face flushing, her eyes full of alarm.

'My, but you're nervous, miss!' A still handsome but heavy woman came into the room. 'I'm sorry if I startled you. I'm Mrs Noble. I expect Mr Greco has told you about us. My husband and I live close at hand.'

'I'm pleased to meet you, Mrs Noble,' Francesca said a little breathlessly. 'I'm Miss Lamb, Francesca Lamb. As you must know, I'm Mr Greco's new housekeeper.'

Mrs Noble hesitated and studied Francesca soberly for a few moments before she said seriously, 'You look very young, Francesca. Too young to be stuck out in a place like this.'

Francesca straightened, and as though her mother gave her a nudge, she said quickly, 'I'd prefer it if you called me Miss Lamb. I'm not afraid of isolation, Mrs Noble. Actually, I prefer it.'

'Then I hope you'll be happy here,' Mrs Noble said in rather offended tones. 'If there's anything you want just ask Mr Noble or me. We'll keep you right. We've been here since Mr Greco took the place over.' With a sigh that seemed to come from her boots she told Francesca, 'We do what we can, but we're getting on a bit. Thomas, that's my husband, is retired. He looks after the grounds and Mr Greco's car. I do what I can in the house. After the city we found Old Beams unbearable for a while, but we're settled now.'

'I'm glad,' said Francesca, giving the woman a more friendly smile. 'I've been working in London,' she volunteered, 'but I felt like a change. I'm afraid I'm not a very social person.'

'But you're young,' Mrs Noble pressed, her large brown eyes expressing concern. 'And I will say this—I wouldn't care for any daughter of mine to be buried here.' She ran her hand through her rather curly grey hair, laughed and said, 'It's not as though Mr Greco will be any help. He never stops working. But then he's a genius—and the world will soon know it.' Glancing back at the door, she added in a lower tone, 'He does go away from time to time, but that's understandable. He may be a genius, but he's a man for all that.' With these words, Mrs Noble's eyes filled with amusement. 'Don't get any ideas, my girl, unless you want him to make a fool of you. You're young, or I wouldn't be saying so.'

Francesca swallowed hard. 'I'm sure that we'll be able to run this house efficiently, Mrs Noble,' she said levelly. 'Mr Greco is paying me a good salary and I intend to earn it.'

'Don't get on your high horse, miss,' Mrs Noble went on, unperturbed. 'Better women than you have thrown themselves at Adam Greco and rued it.'

Now Francesca blushed hard. Mrs Noble began to laugh, but not unkindly. To Francesca's embarrassment she suddenly laid a heavy hand on her arm and said soberly, 'You must be heaven-sent. Adam Greco needs a sensible sort of girl about the place. At this point in his career he doesn't want any distractions—as I said, his mind is full of music at the moment. I'm sure you understand. You look a sensible little creature.' Stamping her way out, she called back from the door, 'We're in the new cottage—I expect Mr Greco told you.'

Francesca did not hear the woman. She only heard the shrill inquiry in her own brain. Was she really so ordinary? Did she really look such a sensible creature? The full weight and significance of Mrs Noble's words tackled her more fiercely now. She went to the wall mirror and frowned into it. Her face was rather long and thin. And she did look a bit peaky. Her hair was ordinary enough; plain brown, a plain style. Yet, she hustled up a defence, Giles Sutherland had once found her distracting enough. He had loved her and had wanted to marry her.

But she would not think of Giles Sutherland. Time had passed. With an air of deliberation, Francesca picked up her case and went out into the hall. All was silent, a kind of sullenness filled the grey air. She made her way upstairs and along the landing to the room which had been allotted to her. It was at the front of the house and staring out of the window Francesca could just see the roof of Thorneyburn Cottage. Her heart beat a little faster and she closed her eyes as an almost uncontrollable desire to rush out of the house and tear across the fields to her own home engulfed her. Instead she gripped the edge of the dressing-table and stood rigidly still. Her mother was no longer there, the cottage was no longer home. Weakly, she turned back into her bedroom. There, everything was the same. The Sutherlands had left everything behind; they had been that type—rich, but uncaring where things or people were concerned.

Pulling herself together, Francesca decided to get ready for bed and then write a long letter of apology to her late employer. She gathered up some of her clothes and toilet bag and hurried along the landing to the bathroom. It was just the same; she stood and smiled at the huge roses on the walls. Half an hour later she was in bed, her dressing gown about her shoulders, while she wrote to Messrs. Paul and Charles Ducal. She would never go back to London, she decided when she

24

finally sealed the envelope down. In a way she had come home. And one day, when she felt a little braver, she would visit her mother's grave.

A few minutes later Francesca stopped writing. She raised her pen and her eyes as the headlights of a car beamed across the wall of her bedroom. She heard the car brake, the wheels grind in the gravel. Then it seemed as if all the doors in the house had opened. The old place shuddered and groaned as though rudely roused from a deep sleep.

Francesca glanced at her travelling clock which now stood by the lamp on the bedside table. It was nine o'clock, and she was tired. She hoped that Adam Greco would not expect her to start entertaining at such an hour. Besides, she reminded herself, she did not begin her duties until the following morning. She lay back against the pillows, listening hard, hoping that she would soon hear the sound of the car skidding off again.

Instead, she heard the sound of raised voices and then footsteps coming quickly up the stairs. She held her breath and wished that she had stayed up and not got into bed so early.

Then came the soft yet impatient tapping at her door and Adam Greco calling, 'Miss Lamb, could I speak to you?'

Was something wrong? Francesca scrambled out of bed and drew her dressing gown about her. 'I won't be a moment,' she called, and nervously smoothed down her hair. Opening the door, she peered out and asked hesitantly, 'Is there something wrong, Mr Greco?'

'Of course not! Why should there be?' Adam Greco's dark eyes skimmed quickly over her and now his eyes registered disappointment. 'I see you've turned in,' he said in a subdued tone. 'I must apologise for getting

25

you out of bed.' Pursing his lips thoughtfully, he added, 'I would have liked you to meet my friends,' his smile was charming, 'and I could have done with a little assistance.'

'Then I'll get dressed and come downstairs again,' Francesca answered in a small voice. 'Is there something you would like me to prepare, Mr Greco?'

He smiled again. 'Just a few sandwiches, cheese and some biscuits. We're going to have a few drinks. Of course you must join us, Miss Lamb. I don't need to be reminded that you don't start working for me until tomorrow.'

'I won't be long,' Francesca said, drawing back, conscious of the gaze which dwelt fixedly upon the soft, pale skin at her throat. 'I'll soon fix something for your guests. Perhaps they would like coffee too?'

'Yes, that would be nice.' Adam Greco seemed lost in thought.

For no reason at all Francesca's heart was pounding. She closed the door and leant against it for a moment. Something in the intensity of his scrutiny had set her foolish blood in full spate. She laughed at herself, but she knew that she was trembling all the same. Then she dressed quickly, putting on a long skirt and an after-eight blouse in white Tricel. After brushing her hair and making up her face, she went downstairs. She did not hurry; her mother had always walked like a duchess.

The sitting room door was open and Francesca could hear happy voices, laughter. Then the door swung back and Adam Greco stood there beckoning to Francesca and calling, 'Come in, Miss Lamb. Come and meet my friends.'

Francesca met the disturbing charm of his smile with a quick, businesslike one of her own. Adam Greco had changed and now he was wearing a casual black velvet tunic with braided lapels and an orchid pink dress shirt. Francesca thought he looked like a prince, but she betrayed no emotion as she stepped forward. But then the man who had been standing by the piano swung round and this time Francesca stood transfixed with shock. Shock registered in every nerve of her body, in every muscle of her face. She turned white. Was it possible?

It was. The man who stood staring back at Francesca with equal alarm in his grey eyes was none other than Giles Sutherland. Stricken, Francesca went on staring at him. Terror thundered in her ears, yet above it she heard Adam Greco say,

'This is my good friend Giles Sutherland, Miss Lamb. Giles, this is Miss Lamb, my new housekeeper.'

Francesca forced a smile. Giles Sutherland's thin, bony hand held her own, his eyes probed her own, but he was not going to give her away, shout out that she was no housekeeper, that she was the girl who had lived for years down in the cottage. The girl he had thrown aside.

'And Celia, his wife.'

Francesca nodded briefly this time, for Celia Sutherland had merely given her a quick uninterested smile of acknowledgment. In that glance though she had seen the discontented curve to the elegant young woman's mouth, her strangely bright green eyes and long hair the colour of withered grass. But she was thinking of Giles. Surely he had been better looking in the old days. How could she have ever imagined she loved a man like that? Now she certainly did not care for his full, pink lips, his thin fair hair and long jaw.

'It seems that you've just arrived in time, Miss Lamb,'

Celia Sutherland remarked, her eyes still on Adam. 'We had dinner early and I'm quite hungry.' She gave Francesca a glance from the corners of her eyes. 'You look very competent,' she said, and her gaze swept over Francesca's rather ordinary clothes. 'I'm sure you'll be able to fix something for us very quickly. If I may,' her eyes caressed Adam Greco again, 'I'd like coffee too.'

'Darling, you may ... You could have the world if it was mine to give.' Adam Greco's lids came down as he spoke.

'It will be one day, so I'll remind you then of your offer,' Celia laughed, and turned tantalizingly to smooth her arm against Adam's.

'If I may suggest it,' he said, and now his dark eyes were wide open again, 'perhaps you could give Miss Lamb a little assistance, Celia. I'm afraid she's not in my employ until the morning. Tonight Miss Lamb is my guest.'

Francesca drew a quick breath of embarrassment. Celia Sutherland did not look like a person who could be relegated to the kitchen. A bony, aristocratic-looking blonde wearing an expensive black dress cut in exquisitely flowing lines and an even more expensive long pearl necklace was by no means the type you told to go away and make some sandwiches. Francesca glanced at Giles and flushed at the long hard look he gave her. Perhaps he read her thoughts? She hoped he did. She felt no enmity, merely shock at seeing him again at Old Beams. If she had ever loved Giles Sutherland, and she felt sure now that she had not, she was cured. He meant nothing to her. All the same, she was grateful that he had not given her away. But then, Francesca thought more coldly, she did not suppose that the wealthy Celia knew anything about the housekeeper's

28

daughter Giles had once wanted to marry.

'All right, Adam,' Celia was saying in too level a voice. 'I'll go along and give Miss Lamb a helping hand. But you must play for us later.' Her tone changed and her voice was softly cajoling again. 'And of course, you must tell us how your work is coming on. I'm looking forward so much to your concert. I'm so proud of you, darling.'

Poor Giles! Francesca turned quickly to go. His wife did not seem to find him very exciting. Plainly Celia Sutherland was attracted to Adam Greco. 'Please don't bother, Mrs Sutherland,' she said pleasantly but firmly. 'I really prefer the kitchen to myself. I'm sure you'll understand.'

Again Celia merely lowered her wonderful eyelashes and made no comment. In the kitchen Francesca stood very still for a moment, thinking not of what she must do, but of the girl she had been three years ago. In her mind's eye she saw herself, painfully thin, white-faced and clinging desperately to an embarrassed young man. 'Don't leave me, Giles,' she heard herself cry. 'Don't leave me. You love me, I know you do. And I love you.' The ghost of her former self made her shiver for a moment, then she pulled herself together and hurriedly made a round of the cupboards. She would make some open sandwiches, she told herself swiftly, fill some vol-au-vent cases. There seemed to be plenty of everything, fresh salmon, tongue, garnish. She set to work quickly.

She heard the door open and without looking round she knew who stood watching her.

'Francesca?'

She closed her eyes. It was Giles and she felt that she could not look at him.

'Francesca, please——'

'Well?' she said shortly, breathlessly. 'I thought you were far away in New Zealand.'

'You knew I would come back.'

Now she turned to stare at him with incredulous eyes. She could not speak.

He came slowly forward, a strange, sad smile on his face. 'I'm back, Francesca,' he said, and the tone of his voice matched his smile. 'I knew I'd find you again.'

Francesca moved hurriedly back as he reached forward to take her hands, her face turning deathly white, her eyes hard.

'You haven't forgotten, Francesca. I know you haven't.' His thin voice was full of anxiety.

'I think you must have forgotten that you have a wife, Mr Sutherland,' Francesca burst out. 'Will you please go? I have work to do.'

'Francesca, don't pretend. You're no housekeeper. I know why you're here. You'd heard that I was back, hadn't you?'

This time she backed away from him. 'Giles,' she whispered brokenly, 'you must be mad. I forgot about you long ago.'

'I don't believe you.' His eyes moved over her. 'You're even more lovely. I never forgot you, not for one moment. You know why I married Celia. It was a business merger, that's all. The two families gathered in quite a harvest.'

'Then you're fortunate. I must work for my living. So if you would excuse me ...'

'I heard that your mother had died, Francesca. I was sorry about that.' He frowned unhappily.

His words froze her this time and she turned to stare in amazement at the man who had caused both her and her mother so much heartache and humiliation. 'Were you really?' she said brokenly. 'Were you really, Giles?'

A stillness filled the room for a few moments and then Giles said quietly, 'Celia was never told about you, Francesca. She has no idea who you are. For the time being I hope we can leave it that way.'

'Of course!' A flush of anger rose to Francesca's face, but she controlled herself, for she did not wish Adam Greco to know of her true identity either. 'I'll keep your terrible secret, Giles ...' she laughed back mockingly, 'for the simple reason that you must keep mine. I'd prefer Adam Greco to think that I was a city miss.'

Giles moved forward again and this time she noticed that his hand was trembling as he laid it upon her arm. 'A secret shared brings people together,' he said in a broken voice. 'We were so close, Francesca. I can't forget.'

At that moment the door opened and Adam Greco walked into the kitchen before Francesca could pull herself together or dismiss the alarm from her eyes.

'I hope we're not imposing upon you too much, Miss Lamb,' he said, and just for a moment his inquiring eyes lay upon Giles. 'I expect you've found by now that my friend is not as domesticated as he would like to make out. Perhaps he's even a hindrance?'

Francesca forced a smile. 'If you'll both go back to the sitting room,' she said with a sigh, 'I'll soon have some trays of refreshment on the way. I do prefer to have the kitchen to myself.'

'It seems that we're all relegated to the kitchen.' Celia Sutherland's voice rose above Francesca's as she glided in and sent a stabbing glance in her direction. 'Just what are you cooking up, Miss Lamb?' she asked, and now her green eyes were glittering. 'I hope you haven't been asked to perform a miracle.'

'Mrs Sutherland,' Francesca said, forcing a smile, 'I'd be grateful if you would take these men away. They're making me begin to doubt my own efficiency.'

'Come along, Adam.' Celia drew Adam away. 'You heard what the girl said. And Giles ...'

Giles Sutherland lingered on until Francesca said sharply, 'You'd better go, Giles. Don't embarrass me.'

'Will you forgive me? Can we be friends?'

Francesca swallowed painfully as she felt his hands lightly cover her shoulders, his breath warm on her neck. 'There's nothing to forgive,' she said in a clipped voice. 'The past is dead, Giles ... and so is my mother. I'm a different person now. I want nothing to do with you. Besides, you seem to forget that you have a wife. She should be your friend—your best one.'

'Then what did bring you back to Old Beams, Francesca?' Giles stood back again, subdued, and again the shadow of sadness crossed his face.

Silently, Francesca turned to stare at him. So Giles had at last learnt that money did not necessarily bring happiness. She felt sorry for him, but not too sorry. As for telling him why she had returned to Old Beams, that was unthinkable. She had returned in search of love ... but not his. She had returned to where she knew her mother's spirit would be. In a strange way she had been almost drawn back.

'Francesca?'

It was a plea, but Francesca merely picked up a tray of vol-au-vents which she had shakily filled and placed it in his hands. 'If you want to do something for me,' she said in a brisk voice that masked her true feelings, 'then take that through to the sitting-room.'

CHAPTER TWO

Alone at last, Francesca got on with her job and after filling two or three plates she set them on a large tray and carried them to the sitting room, pausing at the door for a moment to gather her composure. No one saw her enter the room as Giles and Celia now stood at Adam Greco's side while he accompanied them in a ballad which they all harmonised with an almost professional expertise. Giles had always had a good voice, Francesca remembered. Celia could sing in harmony even if her voice was rather thin and reedy, and as for Adam Greco——! Francesca's throat worked with emotion, her eyelids lowered as she listened to the full, disturbing, rich sweetness of his voice.

Quietly she set the tray down on a table by the fire, then she stood back to listen again. A slow smile came to her lips because she thought Adam Greco looked so darkly stern as he sang, so involved.

As soon as the singing was over Adam Greco stood up, his expression changed, his dark brows raised to Francesca as he called, 'Won't you sing with us, Miss Lamb? You must have some favourite song?'

'I'm sure she has, darling,' Celia cut in before Francesca could answer. 'And I'm sure she sings like an angel. But I'm hungry. And I'm dry too. Adam, be a dear, and get me a drink. Let's have something more cheerful next time. The old house seems a bit glum tonight.'

'What nonsense! How could it be with you in it,

Celia?' With smiling courtesy, Adam Greco moved away to get Celia a drink. Glancing back at Francesca, he called, 'What can I get you, Miss Lamb? A Martini with a hint of lemon?'

'I must see to the coffee,' Francesca said quickly, noticing that Giles had moved away to the shadows.

'Let's have your news, Adam,' Celia was saying. 'You know how terribly interested I am. I just can't wait. And you must tell me what a quartet is, Adam. Someone asked me the other day, and darling, I felt ridiculous when I didn't know.'

'Miss Lamb, do you know what a quartet is?'

With a start, Francesca looked up at Adam Greco.

'Don't be silly, Adam.' Celia sounded impatient, her laugh was forced. 'Do you want to embarrass the girl?'

'I do know what a quartet is,' Francesca said simply. 'My mother didn't play an instrument, but she was a musician all the same. A quartet is a piece written not for a full orchestra but only for four instruments. If one of the instruments is a piano, then it's a piano quartet. More often it's a string quartet.'

'Quite right.' Adam Greco studied Francesca's earnest face, a half puzzled, half pleased smile on his own. 'It's a very difficult piece to compose, I must tell you.'

'Thank you for explaining it so well to me, Miss Lamb.' With a petulant glance, Celia turned back to Adam Greco. 'What about my drink?' she asked in a tone that held just a hint of acidity. 'You haven't forgotten, have you, Adam?'

Francesca hurried to the door, and then saw that Giles had come after her. 'Sit down, Miss Lamb,' he said quietly. 'You must be tired. I don't know what we're thinking about. You've been travelling all day. I'll see to the coffee and brandy.'

'If you're tired,' Celia said in a hard voice and fixing her eyes on Francesca, 'I'm sure we can manage now. You can go to bed.' Turning back to Adam, she taunted, 'What do you think, Adam? Perhaps your housekeeper does look a little pale. My dear husband looks quite concerned for her. I'm sure you won't work her too hard.'

After filling a glass, Adam Greco turned slowly to Francesca and for a moment their gazes clung. Then he smiled and said, 'Miss Lamb does look pale, Celia ... pale and chaste. As though she's only interested in the things of the spirit and doesn't belong to our world.'

'Pale and chaste?' Celia laughed outright as Adam Greco placed a glass in her hands. 'Now tell me,' she insisted playfully, 'how can you possibly tell that a woman is chaste, especially these days?'

'Just as women have their intuition,' Adam Greco said slowly and in a deep, thoughtful tone, 'men too have a way of knowing. But, my dear Celia, you don't really expect me to tell you the secret.' As he spoke he crossed the room softly and, taking Francesca's arm, led her back to a deep-seated chair and gently pressed her into it. 'Sit down,' he said. 'Giles is right, you must be tired. Perhaps my playing may help to relax you. Miss Lamb?'

Francesca looked up. Now Adam Greco was smiling down at her. His smile was like a sudden gleam of sunshine in the dimly lighted room. She felt warmed, almost happy. Suddenly it was as though she had something to live for. She watched him cross to the piano, her heart beating very fast again, her whole being throbbing with a new kind of joy.

The quiet room was filled with music. For Francesca, the melody was like the extension of Adam Greco's smile. All her problems and troubles dwindled into the back of her mind as she sat back to listen. The music filled her heart; evoked for her the sound and smell of the woods and fells she knew so well. She felt the wind stirring in the long grass, she heard the lapping burn, saw the little birds. Her heart was stirred to compassion for all those who also had seen these things and who now lay still beneath autumn's tattered yet still glorious blanket.

'You fell asleep.'

Francesca started up, blinked into Adam Greco's half accusing, half humorous eyes. Somewhere in the room there was the note of mocking laughter.

'I wasted my time!' Adam Greco pursed his lips and shrugged his shoulders, but his gaze was still gentle as it dwelt upon her.

'Oh, no, I didn't!' Francesca sat forward. 'I was wide awake all the time, daydreaming perhaps, but I saw it all.'

'Saw it all?' Adam Greco inclined his head a little and frowned. 'What do you mean, Miss Lamb?'

Embarrassed now, Francesca told him quickly and a little sharply, 'When I listen to music I see things. Your music was delightful, Mr Greco. Therefore I saw the things that delight me most.'

He turned away, a thoughtful gleam in his dark eyes, and then Giles came in with the coffee and Celia said in a loud, clear voice,

'Oh, coffee! Thank goodness. I could do with a stimulant. Bring it over to the fire, Giles.' With a mocking smile she added, 'Sorry I'm so useless, but then my role is to be decorative, isn't it?'

'Of course! And you always are, Celia.' Giles spoke in monotone and his wife, glancing up, laughed at him.

Soon they were sitting before the cheerful log fire chatting, drinking and enjoying the buffet supper which Francesca had made. Francesca sat back, exhausted now, unable to think of anything to say, unable to keep her mind upon what was being said. She noticed the contemptuous glance Celia Sutherland gave her husband now and again and she began to feel just a little sorry for Giles. She noticed too how Celia's bright eyes kept straying to Adam Greco, and she could understand why Giles looked sullen and rather listless.

Then she flinched, because Adam Greco had paused to stare across at her and smile just for her and she realised that he had been studying her for some time. He stood up, but now he turned to Celia. 'And now,' he said, and his mouth pursed into a thoughtful smile as he stared down at her, 'I will play for you.'

'Thank you, Adam.' Her eyebrows arched. 'But before you do,' she said lightly, 'perhaps you would be kind enough to fill my glass. My husband seems to be in some kind of trance.'

Swallowing her dismay, Francesca turned her face away from Giles, who had been watching her intently. Surely, she thought, Giles was not going to give himself away? Then Adam Greco sat down before his piano again, running his fingers in a desultory fashion across the keyboard. As though in some world of his own now, he struck a few chords. A drifting kind of music filled the firelit room; a sonorous, almost sensual sound. Turning her head a little, Francesca saw Celia smile languorously, smile and then stretch out her long, lovely body, her feverishly bright eyes never leaving Adam.

With a feeling of panic, Francesca turned her eyes

to Giles. To her amazement she saw him give his wife a glance as coldly indifferent as that of a searchlight. Francesca fastened her eyes on the luxurious rug before the hearth, then she shut them tight as though in an effort to free herself of the cold reality of life. At that moment it seemed to her that the punishment for Giles Sutherland's crime against her was almost too great. She had never seen a more unhappy-looking man. She pitied him.

'Adam darling, that was superb. Wonderful!'

The tone of Celia's voice made Francesca give her a quick lidded glance, but she quickly looked away again. Celia Sutherland's expression betrayed her; there was no disguising the longing in those green eyes.

'Yes, you are a genius,' Celia went on excitedly. 'And whatever prize you're hoping to win, I'm sure you'll get. Adam, we must celebrate. I must give you a party. Yes, we must celebrate at Thorneyburn House.' With a purring kind of laugh, 'You see how confident I am in your success!'

Peering up again, Francesca saw just how confident Celia was. She positively glowed in the firelight. Her eyes were gloriously green, her lips moist and parted. Her whole demeanour held a blatant message, a message from which Francesca recoiled.

Adam began to play again. This time the notes were poignantly clear. They fell like raindrops into Francesca's tired brain, raindrops which stirred up memories. She drew up her legs and smiled a little. Her mother was calling, 'Francesca! Francesca, my pet, you must get up. It's time for school.'

For a while Francesca was happy in the warm world she had lost. But when she awoke it was with a start. In dismay she sprang to her feet. She stared down at the rug which had fallen from her to the floor.

'What is it?' Adam Greco's voice was deep with concern. 'A dream? Or a nightmare, Miss Lamb?'

Francesca blinked and fought to put her confused thoughts in some kind of order. 'What time is it?' she whispered, staring about the darkened room, conscious now of Adam Greco's hard scrutiny.

'Three o'clock in the morning. The party is over.'

'They've gone?' Francesca thought how silly she sounded.

'Naturally.'

'Then why didn't you wake me?' she asked, braving the intensity of his gaze. 'Why didn't you go to bed, Mr Greco?'

'You looked so happy, I didn't want to disturb you.' He smiled at her extreme youth and added, 'Giles was quite concerned about you. He has a very kindly nature. I'm very fond of him.'

'And Celia?' Francesca asked before she could stop herself. 'Are you fond of her?'

'I'm fond of Celia too,' he said, raising his dark eyebrows in an expression of amusement. 'But that was not what you meant, was it, Miss Lamb?'

'I'm so tired, I don't know what I mean.' Francesca went on shakily. 'I'm just sorry to have kept you out of your bed.' She made an impatient gesture. 'I know nothing about your friends, except that Mr Sutherland looked a little forlorn. Perhaps he should assert himself a little more. Mrs Sutherland struck me as a person with a very strong personality.'

'Too strong for her husband, perhaps.' Adam Greco smiled as he smoothed his solid chin. 'No, we mustn't mistake my friend's good manners for weakness,' he told her. 'But I'm sure you could never mistake kindness for weakness, Miss Lamb.'

'You know nothing whatever about me,' Francesca said in a small voice as she picked up the rug. 'But thank you for playing for me, Mr Greco. I shan't forget that kindness.'

'Nor I the pleasure.' He smiled again. 'Thank you for coming to this out-of-the-way place. I never dreamt that anyone under ninety would turn up. I live like a hermit, but I certainly don't expect anyone else to do so.'

'Perhaps you break out now and again, Mr Greco.' Warily Francesca watched his expression, hoping for some mad reason that he would contradict her statement. He merely smiled again, and taking her arm led her out to the hall.

Nervousness was making Francesca say the wrong thing. Ashamed now, she went quickly away to the shadow of the staircase.

'Miss Lamb?'

'Yes?' She turned back. Adam Greco was standing in the doorway, the light behind him catching his face, the pale silk at his throat making his skin glow even more darkly. His hair gleamed in the light, the unruly wave falling a little over his broad brow again. His eyes glinted curiously. Francesca's gaze moved shyly over the breadth of his chest and then up to the dark column of his throat. Then she saw that he was smiling, in an amused fashion, and embarrassment whipped the colour to her face again. 'Yes?' she said again.

Adam Greco did not answer, he just kept on smiling. Francesca found herself swallowing painfully, her breath coming in ridiculous little spurts. Then she smiled too and said quickly, 'I meant to help, but it seems that I've been a bit of a nuisance. I'm sorry I've kept you out of your bed, Mr Greco.'

'There's no need for you to be sorry,' he said, and moved towards Francesca, his dark eyebrows raised now in some kind of inquiry.

Almost rudely, Francesca drew back, conscious of his powerful masculinity, she felt herself tense.

'You're not afraid of me?' He frowned questioningly. 'You're not going to insist upon a chaperone?' Inclining his magnificent head a little, he asked softly, 'Do I look like a man who would take advantage of being alone in the house with a young woman?'

His eyes were full of dancing lights and before Francesca could answer him she had to take a deep, steadying breath. 'You called me back, Mr Greco,' she said primly. 'What do you want?'

Adam Greco stared down into the upraised eyes which were so full of the solemnity of youth. 'I wanted to tell you,' he said slowly, 'that the Sutherlands have invited you to have dinner at Thorneyburn House next Saturday. Celia said she would leave it to me to persuade you to accept the invitation.'

Again Francesca felt a rush of aggression she did not understand. 'No doubt you've done some persuading in your time, Mr Greco,' she thrust back. 'But I happen to have a mind of my own and I've no intention of going to Thorneyburn House.'

Adam Greco's eyes gleamed. 'But you came here to look after me,' he said softly.

'I was not employed as a chaperone, Mr Greco. Nor did I expect you to concern yourself with my affairs. I'm not lonely, Mr Greco. Please understand that. Neither you or your friends need cater for me.'

He did not speak this time and she caught her breath

as he stood studying her with amused and yet frowning
puzzlement. In the stillness of the softly lighted hall
they stood staring at each other, in surprise, in silence.
Some inexplicable emotion whipped the colour to
Francesca's slim throat and face. I'm crazy, she thought
with rising panic, experiencing the first jolt of her
awareness to Adam Greco's magnificent masculinity;
the dark column of his throat was strong, his shoulders
broad and his hips hard and slim. He moved towards
her and it seemed to her that his eyes were like liquid
fire. She tensed again and drew back.

'You're afraid of me, Miss Lamb. But why?' His
voice was sharper now. 'I can see that I must put your
mind at rest, tell you that you'll be safe enough at Old
Beams with a man whose only love is his work. As for
the dinner party ...' his eyes were smiling again, 'I
would consider it a favour if you would come along.'

'Very well,' Francesca nodded, then turned quickly
to the stairs. 'Goodnight, Mr Greco.'

His words followed her up the stairs. 'We must remember to leave Thorneyburn House by twelve or, I
dare say, you'll turn back into a very formidable housekeeper!'

With her hand on the banister rail, Francesca turned
back. 'You employed a housekeeper,' she told him.
What did you expect, Mr Greco?'

Again he considered her in silence, then he said, 'I
must confess that I had no one like you in mind, Miss
Lamb.' His dark eyes held Francesca's for longer than
was necessary and her heart began to beat fast. Tre-
mulously she asked him,

'Someone less chaste, perhaps?'

He frowned again. 'No,' he told her slowly, 'let's say
someone less sensitive. You see,' his eyes glittered, 'I am

sure that you are sensitive, Miss Lamb.'

Francesca turned and fled before he could continue. Once in her bedroom she quickly closed the door and went straight to the dressing-table where she stood staring into the mirror. Something in Adam Greco's manner had her all worked up; she felt tense, ridiculously excited and alarmed too. Why had the Sutherlands invited her to dinner? She was a housekeeper, not one of their companions now. Were they sorry for her? She braced herself at the idea. Had Adam Greco put it to Celia that she was lonely? Celia would do anything to impress Adam Greco, that was obvious. Or was it Giles? Was he scheming to degrade her yet again? Francesca sighed and sagged a little wearily again. Too late to worry, she had foolishly said she would go now. It was just possible, an unpleasant thought remained to jeer her, that Adam Greco hoped to use her as a kind of shield against his own straying emotions, against the provocation of Celia Sutherland's lovely, lean body, her beautiful green eyes and hair the colour of withered grass.

Once in bed, Francesca sat smiling at her own ridiculous calculations and absently admiring the apricot walls and the heavy peacock blue curtains. She did not think Adam Greco was in love with Celia Sutherland. Hadn't he impressed upon her that his only love was his work? He was a genius, not an ordinary man! A man dedicated to his music. Even if he had put it into the Sutherlands' heads to invite her along, then he was a kindly man. It had been nice of him. No, she did not think he was in love with Celia.

Francesca lay down, but almost immediately she was up on one elbow again, listening intently. Adam Greco was playing again. Gentle sounds filtered through the old house; like kindly spirits they stole into each shadowy corner and alcove; they drifted softly upstairs and into Francesca's room ... and her heart. She lay very still now, imagining that Adam Greco played for her alone. Strong, yet sensitive, kind, a man apart, and yet one who understood. In her mind's eye she saw him seated before his piano, the firelight shining upon his powerful profile, his rich hair and broad brow. Surely, she thought with a kind of panic building up within her again, surely Adam Greco was not in love with his friend's wife? Surely she was not going to be foolish enough to fall in love with such a man, the unobtainable? The very idea made her clench her hands into small fists. She sat up, listening intently to the music now. Then with a long sigh she lay down again. Go to sleep, she told herself.

The next morning she was up at eight o'clock. She was surprised to find that Mr and Mrs Noble had already made their breakfast.

'This is Thomas, Mr Noble,' his wife said, giving the paper her husband was reading a significant smack.

'Morning, miss,' said Mr Noble, pushing the paper away for a moment. 'Nice and bright and crisp, isn't it? This weather suits me. There's not so many of those fearful beasties about.'

'He means midges,' Mrs Noble put in. 'They seem to like Thomas. God knows why, he has no blood!'

Francesca smiled and then set about making her own breakfast; a pot of coffee and a slice of toast. Soon the Nobles left the room, Mrs. Noble calling, 'I'll be upstairs if you want me. I like to get the bedrooms fixed first.'

'We'll have a chat about everything at about ten

o'clock,' Francesca called back firmly. 'We really must get organised, Mrs Noble.'

Mrs Noble shrugged her broad shoulders and then said a bright good morning to Adam Greco, who had just entered the room. Francesca, for some ridiculous reason, felt herself flushing. Desperately she sought refuge before the large stove.

'Good morning, Miss Lamb,' Adam Greco said in a deep but still sleepy voice. 'Did you sleep well?'

Francesca nodded. 'I gather we all have breakfast in the kitchen,' she said quickly.

'Yes, that's right.' He wandered across the room and stood for a few minutes gazing out of the window. 'It's a pleasant room,' he said thoughtfully, his hands buried deep in the pockets of his dark quilted dressing-gown, 'and it has such a wonderful view. I love that great tide of pines and the great rock wall behind it and the clouds that skim over them all.' With a smile he turned back to Francesca. 'How do you feel this morning, Miss Lamb?' he asked in a more lighthearted tone. 'As determined to stay as you were last night, I sincerely hope?'

'I've just arrived at Old Beams, Mr Greco,' she told him nervously, busying herself at the stove. 'Why should I want to run away?'

'Why, indeed!' His steady gaze followed her back to the table. 'I decidedly want to keep you. I've been cured miraculously of my aversion for housekeepers.' He gave her a smile as he sat down. 'I'm quite sure you won't even complain if I glance over a score while I'm drinking my coffee.'

'I'm your housekeeper, Mr Greco,' Francesca laughed back shyly now, and conscious of the fresh tang of his skin and the fact that he was so casually dressed she carefully kept her distance. 'You make me sound like your mother.'

'An impossibility for which I'm more than grateful,' he tossed back. Then he frowned and told her, 'Don't keep darting about, Miss Lamb. You're making me dizzy. Aren't you going to sit down and have something yourself?'

'All right,' she murmured, turning away now so that he could not see her expression, 'I will have some coffee, but in future I'll have my breakfast with the Nobles.'

'Oh, you've seen them.' Adam Greco leant back on his seat to observe her across the table. 'What do you think of them?'

Francesca sipped her coffee, then answered, 'I can see that Mrs Noble has a mind of her own. I think she resents me. She probably thought you were managing very well without a housekeeper. I didn't see much of Mr Noble.'

Adam Greco sighed and returned to his breakfast of grilled ham and kidneys, mushroom and fried egg.

'There's no fruit juice or cereal in the house,' Francesca told him as she watched him eat. 'I must see that they're ordered at once.' Standing up, she asked, 'Would you like some fresh coffee?'

'I think I would,' he answered her, and as she moved away his dark, thoughtful eyes followed her once again. She was like a lovely ghost from the nineteenth century, he thought curiously, pale and fragile, sober-eyed and lovely as she attended to his needs in the most prim and business-like manner. Slim, erect back, slender neck and shining, swaying hair, eyes which could widen like those of a startled fawn.

'Miss Lamb!' he called suddenly, and with a slow

46

smile on his lips he watched Francesca turn round to face him.

'Yes?' she gulped, conscious of some strange curiosity in the dark eyes that watched her. 'Yes?' she said again.

'Oh nothing,' he murmured, and he smoothed his dark chin and frowned at the table as though to suppress a smile. 'Carry on.'

Stirring the coffee, Francesca thought of the man who sat watching her from the table. For a moment she wished she could find some displeasing aspect about him; something which would immediately dash out the kindling of warmth which he had roused within her. She would not be duped by pride again, she told herself. Self-respect must save her from making a fool of herself once again. Her mother had been a housekeeper in the Sutherlands' household; she herself was housekeeper now for Adam Greco. Because he had a kindly spirit and was at times perhaps a little lonely he was treating her as a contemporary. Indeed, he was using her, she reminded herself coldly. All the same, in her mind's eyes she saw Adam Greco's darkly brilliant eyes, eyes which could be cheerful or heavy with reflective melancholy. She saw his mouth, wide and sensual, and turned away quickly.

She poured out some coffee for him and then some for herself and sat down again. For a while they were silent. When the clock in the hall struck nine Adam Greco looked up and said, 'That was wonderful, Miss Lamb. If I write a masterpiece today I'm sure it will be due to your excellent cooking.' He sat back again, frowned a little and inclined his head to one side as he observed Francesca in silence for a few moments. Then tiny flames of light leapt from the smouldering of his eyes and he leant forward a little and said, 'Please allow me to call you Francesca. It's such a lovely name and it suits you well. Somehow I can't get used to saying Miss Lamb.'

Aware of a restriction in her throat, Francesca stood up quickly. His kindness stirred emotion within her; she could not answer him.

'I take it then that you don't approve?'

He was amused now and she heard his chair scrape back as he stood up.

'As you haven't answered me,' he teased, 'then I'll take my choice. And now I must give White Cloud her morning canter. I suggest you have a short walk before you do anything, Francesca. The country air will soon whip some colour into those pale cheeks, some gaiety perhaps into your rather sober heart. You really mustn't take life so seriously, you know. You must never expect the worst, always the best.'

Rooted to the spot, Francesca watched him quickly stride from the room, then slowly she turned to the window. At one time she had lived in a fantasy world, she had believed in dreams. She had made her mother believe in them too. Now her mother was dead and there were no more dreams, only sadness in her eyes, a sadness which Adam Greco had detected. But he knew nothing of her, he lived in a different world. By the time he was thirty-five he would be world-famous. No one would trample upon him. He called her Francesca because he liked the name. A smile touched Francesca's lovely mouth. It was not exactly protocol, but the idea wrapped about her like a warm cloak. For a few moments she was filled with gladness.

She cleared the breakfast table, stacked the dishes and then decided that she would take Adam Greco's advice and go for a walk. Yes, she would fill her lungs with fresh fell air. She hurried into the hall and picked up her green corduroy jacket. Pulling it on, she stared up at the grandfather clock which she had loved for so many years. She looked at the painted bird and then at the large Roman numerals and for a moment her mother seemed to be there beside her in the quiet hall, teaching her to read the time, urging her on. It was a pleasing, homely piece of furniture and almost reverently Francesca reached out to smooth her fingers over the satin surface of the old oak. Then, with a sigh, she ran out of the house.

The Nobles were arguing at the entrance. Francesca merely gave them a brief nod, her thoughts still far away. Half way down the drive she paused to glance back at the old house, then more determinedly she hurried out of the gates, crossed the lane, climbed the fence and made her way down over the field towards the old Wanny railway line. She recalled her mother telling her about the track and how it had been pulled up; how all the people for miles had come to see the last train and the track that would never come back. Sad, she thought, as she clambered up the embankment and over the line, down again on to the field on the other side. Then she began to run. She ran as she had done when she was a child, smiling, with her long hair streaming behind her. She ran past a still, sober-eyed cow, then past some grazing sheep. Then she began to walk slowly again, for she had reached the little valley, the dell through which the stream ran and upon whose slopes the old Thorneyburn Cottage was built. Grave-eyed, she crossed the stream, making her way up the bank to the cottage which had once been her home.

There was a high grey stone wall about the sturdy little house and reaching the back gate, Francesca could see that a green fungus had already taken possession of the walls. With fast beating heart she opened the gate and was just about to try the back door when she heard voices.

She stopped dead, her heart hammering fearfully now. Was she imagining things? She gulped nervously, then strained her ears again. No, someone was there at the front of the house. She could hear their deep conversational murmuring. Someone laughed, and something about the shrill high laugh froze Francesca's blood. Surely not? Surely she had not strayed into a place of secret rendezvous?

With a feeling of alarm and desperation, she made her way silently along the side of the house, then paused at the beech hedge which ran from the house to the outer wall. Unseen, she listened again, and now she was quite sure. There was no mistaking Celia Sutherland's laughter, or Adam Greco's deep rich voice. Warily, Francesca raised her head above the leafless hedge, then dodged down again, her blue eyes wide with alarm. What could she do? Somehow she had to get away unobserved. For it was Adam Greco who leant against the small garden gate at the front of the house, while Celia stood before him, the sunlight on her blonde hair, her eyes shining as she raised her hands to smooth the lapels of his fine tweed jacket.

'Darling, must I be such a problem?' came Celia's plaintive voice. 'You must admit that I've been a help to you.'

Shocked, Francesca raised her head again, and just in time to see Celia press her lovely lean body hard against Adam Greco's. Transfixed, she watched them. She heard Adam Greco say something and then Celia was against the wall and Adam's dark hair seemed to mingle with Celia's long fair tresses. They moved again, and now Francesca saw the way in which Adam Greco's mouth lingered across Celia's face and down to her throat.

She sank back like someone who had just taken poison. She had imagined that sympathetic listening was enough for this man of genius. Hadn't Mrs Noble told her that Adam Greco was a man as well as a genius, that from time to time he went away? With whom? Celia Sutherland? Surely not? Weak with shock, Francesca crept back to the gate. She struggled with it, sensibly at first, quietly, then as though she had lost control of herself. Then in terror she turned to the man who called, 'Hello there! What are you doing down here?'

'I'm trying to open this gate,' Francesca faltered as Adam Greco strode along by the wall towards her. 'It looked such a sweet cottage. I saw it was empty and I decided to look in.'

'So you've just arrived?' His voice was polite but slightly strained.

Francesca nodded and then lowered her eyes lest he should read the contempt which she knew now filled them. Or was it pain?

Then Celia came round the corner smoothing back her long hair, her eyes shining. 'Oh, it's you,' she called rather coldly. 'What are you doing so far away from the house? I always thought town girls were scared to take more than a few steps in the country.' She laughed shrilly and her eyes strayed to Adam, who was studying Francesca with sober eyes.

'There's no need for you to walk back,' Adam said abruptly. 'White Cloud has a strong back. I'll give you a ride back, Francesca.'

'Francesca!' Celia's slim throat worked and her eyes glittered coldly now. 'You've only been here a few hours,' she laughed mockingly, 'and it seems you have a protector already, Miss Lamb.'

Francesca turned to Adam Greco and looked directly at him. 'I'm enjoying the fresh air,' she told him. 'And I would like to look in this cottage. After that I'll walk quickly back to Old Beams. Please, ignore me and get on with whatever you were doing.'

'Now isn't that kind?' Celia's voice rose again. 'You don't need to carry the girl home, Adam.'

This time Adam Greco ignored Celia. He whistled for his pony and White Cloud came trotting around the corner and up to the gate. Without a word Adam Greco swept the unsuspecting Francesca from her feet and placed her lightly in the saddle. 'At times I do give the orders,' he laughed, then he sprang up behind her, holding her fast with one hand as he picked up the rein with the other. 'Don't get any wrong ideas about me, Francesca.'

She would not, thought Francesca hotly, and she steeled her emotions against the strong arm which held her firmly. White Cloud set off at a steady canter and Adam Greco called back, 'We'll look forward to Saturday, Celia. It seems a pity that Francesca and I must get back to our work.'

'It is,' Celia laughed back mockingly. 'But then I'm sure the devil would never waste time tempting Miss Lamb.'

'But you're not yet sure about me, Celia?' Adam turned White Cloud and then circled away again.

'Who could ever be sure about you, Adam?'

'Who indeed?' he chuckled as White Cloud passed Celia.

Francesca heard Celia call for her own mount, but she could no longer think of anything except the closeness of Adam Greco and the way in which he held her firmly and hard against himself. She could feel his warm breath on her neck where her hair parted, his muscled thigh against her own soft one. She caught her breath, then went hot again as her sweater parted from her jeans and she felt the contact of his firm fingertips against her skin.

They had started downhill towards the stream when Francesca heard the quick thud of hoofs behind them and glancing back saw that Celia was hard after them. She drew her breath again when Celia's mount skimmed dangerously close.

'That was dangerous,' Francesca breathed, 'I hope she won't do it again.'

'She will,' said Adam Greco, seemingly unperturbed. 'But don't panic. I won't let you fall, Francesca.'

Celia came again, thundering across the rough turf and once again almost crashing into White Cloud.

'Stop her! Stop her!' Francesca cried out fearfully now, her body taut, her face hidden against Adam Greco's supporting arm. 'Please, she's dangerous.'

'Yes, she is,' Adam Greco said in a reflective tone once they had reached the ford. 'Celia's dangerous all right. Excitingly so.'

CHAPTER THREE

FOR the rest of the day Francesca busied herself about the house and programmed the work for the rest of the week. She had a long talk with Mrs Noble, convincing the stony-eyed woman that although she was not to be overburdened by work, she would have to do some. Later, Francesca felt that she had perhaps been a little sharp, but she had felt restless and uptight all day. Seeing Celia and Adam Greco in such an embrace had done something to her. And she had not liked the way in which Adam Greco had lifted her down from White Cloud and then gone off without even a word. Now her thoughts turned to Giles, and the hatred she had once felt for him gave way to a kind of pity. She was also conscious of a vague kind of guilt, for she knew that Giles had never once stirred up her emotions in the way Adam Greco had that very morning. And he had merely been giving her a ride back to the house. Francesca went hot again as she remembered his arm about her waist, the dark wrist, the pressure of his fingertips against her skin. He had merely held her firmly, she told herself, just as he would have held a dog or a sack of corn.

What Adam Greco did was no business of hers! She was not there to condemn, or judge him morally. She was there to run his house and see that he got his evening meal. The fact that she had promised to have that meal with him was now the reason for her nervousness. She wished that she had been sensible enough to stay in her place. Her mother had so often said, 'Guard your own privacy, Francesca. That's something we all have. Never lose your self-respect.'

But she belonged to a new generation, Francesca argued with herself as she set the dining-room table for two. Young people no longer believed in the caste system. In the country, though, it was still there. The villagers still kept to their village while the county set still kept high walls about their houses, and paid for a church pew to keep them close to God yet still at a safe distance from the common herd.

Once everything was in order for their evening meal, Francesca went off to wash and change. She made up her face a little more carefully than usual and put on a long, fine tweed skirt and a cream crêpe blouse with sleeves which flowed into a soft fullness. A wide suede belt accentuated her neat waist and a long pearl necklace added a hint of elegance. She did not look too drab, she decided after a last frown at herself in her dressing-table mirror. Not in Celia's class, of course, but at least she had made an effort.

When Francesca went back to the dining-room she saw that Mr Noble had built up the fire in the grate of the beautiful black marble fireplace and that the curtains had been drawn. It was an elegant yet cosy room with a low beamed ceiling and dark and medium red striped wallpaper. A luxurious Persian carpet covered most of the floor and the furniture was heavy and antique. A huge contemporary-looking lamp stood by the round rosewood table. The firelight cast a rosy glow over everything.

Adam Greco came in as the clock struck seven o'clock. 'This is wonderful,' he said, pausing by the table. His gaze lingered upon Francesca and he smiled slowly as he told her, 'You look very charming too, Francesca. I can see that I'm going to look forward to my evening meal.' He turned away. 'Let me get you a drink,' he said, strolling over to the small Georgian cabinet which stood in one of the alcoves. 'A dry Martini? Something simple?'

Something simple? Yes, thought Francesca, and she lowered her eyes after nodding to him. For she was a simpleton. Only a simpleton would entertain the thoughts that were dashing about her brain. Only a simpleton would tremble the way she was doing just because a man had come into the room.

'Have you had a good day?' she asked rather stiffly, as he returned with her drink.

'Extremely successful.' Dipping his brows a little, he inquired, 'And you, Francesca, have you had a good day? Did it seem endless?'

'Of course not.' Francesca held her glass with both hands. 'I've been very busy. Time has flown. And now if you'll sit down I'll serve dinner.' Charmingly she placed her own glass to one side.

Adam Greco took it up again and placed it back in her hands. 'There's no hurry,' he said, and his eyes were bright with amusement. 'Please finish your drink. We have the whole evening before us, Francesca. Relax, I'd like you to do that. You always look so startled. Do I really make you feel so nervous?'

'I'm certainly not nervous,' Francesca answered. 'I'm merely anxious that you enjoy the meal I've prepared. It happens to be at its best at this moment. I'll enjoy my Martini with it.'

'Very well.'

Francesca smiled more happily as the distance stretched out between them and Adam Greco sat down

56

at the far side of the table. 'I've prepared one of the dishes my mother used to love,' she told him. 'Braised rabbit with mushrooms and parsnips. But first of all you must have some of my home-made soup. You work hard, Mr Greco, and I must feed you well.'

'You mean I must work harder,' Adam Greco said absently, as he watched Francesca serve the food. 'I'm afraid I've been neglecting my work of late. Perhaps I should really be cast away on a desert island. I'm ashamed to admit that I can be distracted.'

'When is your next concert?' Francesca asked as she set down a bowl of soup before him, and then moved off to serve one for herself. 'I'd love to hear about it. And I promise not to distract you at all. Once I get the run of the house you need never see me.'

'Are you such a mouse?' he laughed, and then leaning forward a little peered across the table at Francesca. 'You need not hide from me, Francesca. As for distracting me,' his mouth quirked at one corner, 'I'm sure you're much too nice a girl to do that.'

Francesca felt as if someone had thrown cold water over her. It seemed that Adam Greco shared Mrs Noble's view; she was not the type to distract a man. She got up and took the bowl from him.

'I fancy I've got myself a splendid cook as well as a housekeeper,' he laughed gently. 'I enjoyed that very much, Francesca.' He sighed then and raised his eyebrows. 'But if only you would smile! Is this house so oppressive?'

His smile set her heart beating fast again and Francesca hurried away to serve the next course. Surely she had not fallen in love with Adam Greco at first sight; surely that was not possible? Yet why had his words so much power, power to hurt or elate? And why had his touch had so much effect upon her? Upstairs that morning she had even searched her skin for the imprint of his fingers. But she could not rid her mind of the picture of him kissing Celia Sutherland. Was she really so much attracted to a man who could readily make love to his friend's wife?

'There is something wrong, Francesca.' He looked up at her as she came to his side. 'You're tired. You haven't been out tramping the countryside again, have you?'

'No,' Francesca whispered. 'I've been much too busy in the house.'

'You seem to like walking, Francesca. Perhaps you're even annoyed at me for sweeping you off your feet this morning?'

'I was a little afraid,' she told him with a nervous laugh. 'I'm not the riding type. In fact it was the first time I've ever ridden on a horse.'

'You were safe enough.' He cast an appreciative eye upon the plate before him. 'You liked Thorneyburn Cottage?' he asked, rather absently. 'It's a quaint place.'

'I'd like to live in a cottage like that,' Francesca told him as they went on with their meal. 'I thought it was beautiful.'

'What? With damp walls and no mod cons? I'd hardly say Thorneyburn Cottage was the place for a girl like you, Francesca.' He frowned at her in surprise.

Warily Francesca ventured, 'Does Mrs Sutherland like the cottage? I thought perhaps she'd been looking over it. It's obviously empty.'

'I don't suppose she noticed it.'

'If I had the money,' Francesca told him solemnly, 'I would buy that cottage.'

'You amaze me.' He smiled again. 'You seem determined to bury yourself in the country, Francesca. I must say that at your tender age it does seem rather strange.' His eyes narrowed a little as he gave Francesca a long assessing look. 'Perhaps you already know of someone who would enjoy living in such a place with you?'

'Not at all,' Francesca returned promptly. 'I suppose I've just fallen in love a little with the place. I like everything about it.'

'But you haven't seen inside it?' Adam Greco's brow puckered questioningly again. 'I met you struggling with the gate, remember?'

'I like its position,' Francesca told him quietly and finally, then they ate in silence again for a while.

Adam Greco got up, smiling now and saying, 'Let's take our coffee into the sitting room. I don't know about you, Francesca, but I feel in the mood for some music. And that,' he told her with eyebrows raised, 'is a compliment. There's something very restful about you, you know. I noticed it at once. It was almost as though you were a natural part of this country scene. You fit in. You remind me of one of those solitary and softly quivering little birds I so often see perched on a willow stem.' His gaze followed her as she began to busy herself with the trolley, her face averted. 'So,' he went on, 'will you please leave that and come and join me. Mrs Noble will clear away.'

'All right.' Francesca took up her cup and saucer and went ahead of him, determined that he would not see the colour which had rushed to her face, the pleasure which she knew shone in her eyes.

'Sit down,' he said, coming into the room behind her and then hurrying ahead to push an easy chair a little closer to the hearth. 'I don't need to tell you to sit still, Francesca. You're not the fidgeting type, thank God.'

'Is Mrs Sutherland a fidgeting type?' Francesca found herself asking before she could stop herself.

Adam Greco paused, then turned to stand with his back to the fire. 'Celia?' he murmured. His dark eyes gleamed and he turned to face the fire. 'Mrs Sutherland is a very sophisticated woman,' he said thoughtfully as he stared down into the leaping flames. 'No, I can't imagine Celia fidgeting.' He laughed and straightened up. 'She's a restless filly, all the same,' he said. 'Perhaps she feels a trifle boxed in at Thorneyburn House. I wouldn't say that Celia was a true countrywoman.'

'What would you say about her?' Francesca's voice shook a little, but she forced a smile to her lips. 'She's certainly beautiful. Most attractive.'

'Oh, most! I'd say Celia would be an asset to most men. Yes, that's what I would say about my friend's wife.' Adam Greco lit a cigar now and in the manner of a man who had something pressing upon his mind he began to wander up and down, away from the fire and back again. To Francesca's embarrassment, he stopped suddenly and stood gazing down at her without saying a word.

'Is there something wrong?' she whispered. 'Is there something troubling you?'

'Why should anything trouble me?' His eyes softened and grew reflective. 'But I have the distinct feeling that something is troubling you, Francesca. If there is, then you must tell me about it.' A mischievous smile touched his lips and again sparks of humour leapt into his dark eyes. 'I'm more than willing to act as your confessor.'

Francesca sat back in her chair. 'I'd much prefer you to play for me,' she told him, and this time her own smile was both shy and mocking. 'I assure you that nothing troubles me.'

'Good, I'm glad to hear it. I'd got the distinct notion that I could well be harbouring a criminal.' His voice was teasing now. 'Criminals are always anxious about other people.'

For a disconcerting moment Francesca's eyes met his and then to her relief he turned and strode over to the piano.

Francesca forgot Celia Sutherland and sat spellbound as she listened to Adam Greco's playing. She felt again some strange stirring of joy within her, a tenderness almost for the man whose music now evoked all that she knew to be beautiful. A melody both poignant and subtle filled the room with sweetness and her heart with memory. Her eyelids grew heavy and eventually her eyes closed as Adam caught the whole beauty and dignity of the moonlit landscape in his web of notes. She opened her eyes again and sat forward a little, staring at the elegant figure so lost in his playing, so far away in a remote world of his own imagining. She caught her breath. It was true; nothing, no one could bring to this man more joy than his own music.

When the music stopped the room was strangely still and silent. Francesca held her breath, afraid to intrude into Adam Greco's magic world, afraid to distract him.

He swung round on the piano stool and she saw that his eyes were brilliant with excitement.

'I have it now,' he breathed. 'Yes, Francesca, I have it now.' Some inner elation illuminated his dark countenance. He sprang up. Then his expression changed. For a moment he looked almost angry. 'Are you asleep?' he asked, and his voice was distinctly hard, impatient.

'Are you dreaming again, Francesca Lamb? Perhaps of some love you have lost?'

Francesca sprang up, her eyes hot now, tears not far away. 'Yes, you're right,' she said levelly. 'I was dreaming of a love I've lost. I'm a silly, pathetic creature. I can't think why you insist upon entertaining me.'

'I wish I knew.'

She raised her eyes and met his. Their gazes clung in a communion of understanding. 'Your music was beautiful,' she told him in a soft voice. 'If I was dreaming, I was only dreaming of the loveliness you conjured up. I was out there beneath the moon. I saw it all.'

He reached out to take her hand and then to her embarrassment and shock he drew her a little closer. 'As well as everything else, Francesca,' he said in his deepest voice, 'you are a perfect audience. For that, I must pay tribute,' and gently raising her chin with the back of his dark hand he purposefully pressed his lips to hers.

Francesca drew back. She could not speak, astonishment held her transfixed. Adam Greco caught her hand and clasping it warmly between his own he frowned a little and peered down a little more closely into her sober eyes. 'A respectable tribute,' he told her, and now his eyes gleamed, 'for a most respectable young lady.'

Francesca pulled herself out of what she felt to be some kind of trance. Adam Greco had kissed her as he would have kissed a maiden aunt, and for some reason she felt bitterly humiliated—wounded almost, certainly very angry. It had been no such mean blessing he had bestowed upon the sophisticated and not so very respectable Celia. For one moment she wanted to fling her arms about his neck and kiss him with all the wild abandon she suddenly felt. Instead, she turned quickly away from him, trying desperately to look as though she was well used to such tributes. She tried even more fiercely to keep calm when her whole being throbbed with some agonizing kind of excitement.

'We must have a nightcap,' Adam Greco said, as he moved away to a small table where a decanter and glasses stood on a tray. 'You're not going to bed yet, Francesca. I insist that you sit down.' He smiled gently at her sober profile. 'If I must assure you again, then I'll say that I have nothing but your good in mind. You're a very nice girl, Francesca Lamb.' Pressing a glass into her hands, he said again, 'Sit down and smile. Just be yourself, Francesca.'

Francesca sat down and then to her surprise he changed his mood and asked almost abruptly, 'What do you think of my friend Giles? I could see that you really impressed him. I'm afraid Celia is a bit too clever for Giles at times. She has a strong personality.'

'Hasn't Mr Sutherland?'

Adam Greco settled himself in the opposite chair before the fire, and gazing into the fire, twirling his glass between his fingers, he said thoughtfully, 'Giles is a very different type. He has his points. I just wish Celia would be appreciative of them.'

'You sound concerned.' Francesca sipped her drink and stared hard into the fire.

'Perhaps,' Adam Greco said dreamily. 'Giles is a kindly man, and Celia is a tigress.' He laughed softly and stirred in his seat, his thoughts far away. 'Poor Giles has rather a weak chest,' he began again after a while. 'And Celia, I'm afraid, has no patience. Still, I hope they'll both manage to hear me play in Edinburgh next month.'

'They're both musical, then?' Francesca tried to draw him back. 'They appreciate what you're doing?'

But Adam Greco was far away again, his glass empty now and resting on the arm of the chair, his fingers lightly about it, his gaze deep in the dancing flames. Francesca watched him closely and soon she saw his eyelids droop and within minutes she knew that he was asleep. She got up quietly and crossing the floor stood looking down at him. Her gaze dwelt softly upon the elegant yet strong hand which held his glass, the heavy eyelids so thickly and silkily lashed. His hair too, she noticed, had a boyish ruffle to it and for a moment she was tempted to run her fingers through it.

She stood back, her heart beating fast again as a smile stirred Adam Greco's wide mouth. Then she heard him mutter, 'Damn you, Celia! Damn you!'

So it was Celia who tortured this man! Francesca drew up stiffly and an uncanny and unreasonable fury gripped her. She spun about now and left the room swiftly, determined to think of nothing but her work in future.

For the rest of the week both Francesca and Adam Greco plunged themselves into hard work. Dust removed, curtains washed, cupboards cleared out, Old Beams began to breathe more easily. Most days Adam had little to say, but Francesca found herself standing still every now and again to listen spellbound as the house filled with rich and evocative harmonies. She got to know Adam Greco's moods; to her sensitive ear she knew exactly how he felt. Sometimes his hands plunged madly over the keys and she knew that he was entreating sounds that would not come. At other times she knew that he smiled as he played and that the melody lazing through his brain pleased him. Always they had their evening meal together, usually a nightcap too, but for some reason now Adam had little to say. At times Francesca wondered if he now regretted the need for a housekeeper. She looked at him, but when he looked at her he seemed to look right through her. Yet in some strange way, Francesca was happy. Each afternoon she walked over the fields and down to the old cottage. In some strange way too, she never felt alone ... her mother's comforting spirit was always with her, she told herself.

On the Friday afternoon the telephone rang and she hurried into the hall to answer it.

It was Giles Sutherland and he said at once, 'Oh, it's you, Francesca. Is Adam busy?'

'He's always busy at this time of day,' she told Giles shortly. 'You know that.'

He ignored her outburst. 'How are you?' he asked. 'I hope the maestro is looking after you.'

'I'm looking after him,' Francesca returned shortly again. 'That's what I'm paid to do, Mr Sutherland.'

'I hear Adam is bringing you over on Saturday night.'

'That's right. Your wife has invited me.'

'I hope we're all going to be friends. I certainly feel as though I need one.'

Something in his tone made Francesca frown. 'You have your wife, Giles,' she said quickly, trying to keep the old bitterness from her voice. 'Surely she is your best friend.'

This time he did not answer and she said impatiently, 'Are you still there, Mr Sutherland?'

'Yes, I'm here, Francesca. Please don't call me Mr Sutherland. Honestly, I can't bear it.'

'Do you want to speak to Mr Greco?' Francesca asked shakily. 'I can get him.'

'You know, I think you could,' Giles' voice came back

with a significance that made her flush. 'And I would deserve watching you go to my best friend. Fortunately the scales of justice are not well balanced.'

A door opened off the hall and Francesca nervously put the receiver down.

'Wrong number?' Adam Greco inquired as he strode into the kitchen.

'No. It was Mr Sutherland,' she told him as she hurried after him. 'He just rang to ask if I was going over on Saturday.'

'And you said you were?' His eyes were steadily questioning.

'I did.'

'Good!' Absently he added, 'We should have a pleasant evening. Although, God knows, I really can't afford the time.'

'Isn't your work going well, Mr Greco?'

'There's something missing,' he told her as he studied the tiled floor. 'I haven't got it yet, Francesca. But I will. I must.'

She noticed that he was trembling and she asked in a small voice, 'Don't you think you're working too hard?'

The sound of her concern brought him back to reality. He ran a hand over his eyes, sighed deeply and then gave her a smile. 'I'm sorry,' he said gently. 'You must forgive me if I've been somewhat remote this week, Francesca. But never mind, we may yet be celebrating with champagne.'

Alone again, Francesca began to prepare an autumn salad. Poor Giles, she thought. Obviously he was not happy. As for Celia Sutherland, she was a tigress all right. And clever—she would not dream of divorcing a rich husband for a man on the verge of fame. She would wait, give Adam his chance ... and then pounce. A divorce at such a critical time would ruin Adam Greco and they were both far too discreet and sophisticated to act so rashly.

It was underhand all the same, and Francesca could not help frowning and once again feeling sorry for Giles. He was pathetic, she thought. How could she have ever imagined herself to be in love with such an insipid man?

He had eyes—he must know what was going on. Or was she herself imagining it all? It was quite possible that Celia Sutherland flirted outrageously with all men. No, she had seen her in Adam Greco's arms. Celia, alas, was too lovely for any man to turn down.

It was with a heavy heart that Francesca dressed for the dinner party the following evening. Yet she had just a hint of aggression in her manner. She was determined not to fade out completely beneath Celia Sutherland's bright beam. She wore her long green velvet skirt and a white chiffon blouse with green embroidery worked on the cuffs and yoke. A bronze clasp fastened the wide belt about her waist and picked up the colour of her brown hair. She was wearing more make-up than usual, a misty blue eye shadow and false lashes. She could never hope to eclipse the aristocratic Celia, but all the same she did not intend to look dull.

Standing before her mirror, Francesca lowered her long lashes, moved her head a little so that her shining locks swayed provocatively and smiled. She was quite pleased with the effort. If only Adam would come in and kiss her now!

She was being fanciful again. Hadn't her mother warned her? It was almost as though her mother stood at her side now. Never be discontented, Francesca heard her say. The better your life, the more you must be in fear of losing it all, Francesca. Never envy anyone. Francesca frowned at her reflection now. Her brow puckered a little as though in some kind of reply. She could never envy anyone, she told herself, but she could love anyone she pleased, providing, of course, that they never knew her secret. Closing her eyes, she thought of Adam Greco's light kiss again and sighed. Never in all her dreams had she expected an employer so disturbingly attractive, one so strong and yet so agonisingly gentle at the same time.

She met him in the hall and in his dark elegant suit and cerise-coloured dress shirt she thought he looked like a Spanish count; elegant, artistic, masterful. By the way he narrowed his eyes at her it seemed as though he had something on his mind. He gave her a long curious look, but to her chagrin made no comment upon her appearance. She moved towards the light a little and still he made no comment. 'Is there something wrong?' she asked, trying to keep disappointment from shadowing her eyes. 'Is there something I can do?'

'There is,' Adam said slowly, and now his eyes looked deep into hers. 'You can call me Adam. There now, it's an order. I insist upon it.'

Francesca felt her blood warm. She moistened her lips and then told him with just a hint of provocation, 'I will, but just for this occasion. I certainly don't feel in a housekeeping mood tonight.'

'You certainly don't look like a housekeeper,' Adam returned in a low voice. 'But then you never do, Francesca.'

She laughed almost gaily as they went out of the house together. 'It all depends on what your housekeeper image is,' she told him. 'You must be a very old-fashioned man, Mr Greco.'

'Adam,' he corrected as he took her arm and steered her towards the car. 'An old-fashioned name,' his fingers turned more deliberately about her arm, 'but I assure you I'm by no means an old-fashioned man. You must know that, Francesca.' As he eased himself into the driving seat alongside her, he leant towards her a little. 'For instance, that perfume you're wearing—it's distinctly outdated. I must remember to buy you something more suitable, something less round and smooth. You're by no means a full woman yet, Francesca.'

'And I suppose Celia Sutherland is,' Francesca said tightly, angry because she knew he was right. Someone had given her the perfume years ago. Because he did not answer her at once she went on hotly, 'Or mustn't I ask questions about Mrs Sutherland?'

'Ask away,' he said levelly, as they drove out of the gates. 'If you're really interested, I'll tell you all I know about Celia.' He laughed and then went on in a more thoughtful tone, 'I know this, Celia never makes a mistake where perfume is concerned. But then Celia is a woman in the full sense of the word.'

'Then we mustn't keep her waiting,' Francesca said a little too sharply, the pleasure she had felt fading out of her as she realised that Adam's preoccupation with Celia was affecting his driving.

Without a word he put his foot down on the accelerator and for a while they drove in silence, each lost in their own thoughts.

Thorneyburn House stood on high ground about four miles to the east of Old Beams. Francesca remembered the great black fortress; the granite block which rose from within high, impenetrable walls. As a child she had crept by the place and glanced up in terror at the jet statue of an eagle which someone had had set on the edge of the roof.

Adam got out of the car and opened the great wrought iron gates which for so many years had always been shut to her.

'It's quite a place,' he commented, as he returned to her. 'Of course the Sutherlands are wealthy landowners. The farmhouse and the cottages are quite a distance from the house, a mile or so down the road.'

Francesca knew where they were and this time she made no comment. She had often walked over with her mother to see one of the women who had lived in the cottages.

'Here we are.'

Adam's words jerked her back to the present, and with a feeling of apprehension she straightened up and stared across the lawns which were flooded with light from the windows. In no time she was out of the car and Adam was guiding her across the gravelled fore-court to the entrance. Then they were in the hall, a spacious elegant hall with a number of high double doors leading from it.

One of the doors opened and Celia Sutherland appeared.

'Darling!' she cried, and came forward to kiss Adam swiftly. 'I'm so pleased to see you.' She stood back to look at him and as Francesca watched it seemed to her that they shared a moment of intense excitement; some secret and subtle communication. Ill at ease and feeling totally ignored, Francesca turned away. But Adam's hand was turning firmly about her arm again and Celia Sutherland said, 'And Miss Lamb! How are you?'

'Very well.' Francesca could barely hear her own voice above the angry thudding of her heart. Without a smile she stared back at Celia, painfully acknowledging to herself that the woman did look stunning in peacock blue evening trousers and a matching velvet tunic which was belted about her waist. She wore a fine silk scarf about her neck and high platform shoes. Her hair was drawn back to accentuate her aristocratic bone structure. She was perfectly made up and the bed of shadow about her eyes was highly dramatic. Francesca wondered why she had bothered with her dreamy blue shadow. Indeed, why she had come at all? Beside Celia Sutherland she did look dull. She was beginning to feel a little dull too.

But the house was interesting ... and it had been good of Celia to invite her, whatever her intention. They followed Celia into a room which took Francesca's breath away. It was a spacious room with long windows and furniture in a blend of old and new. A low chrome and glass table stood in the centre of a brilliant rug and the large leather settee and chairs were pushed well back against the pale ochre walls. The old fireplace had been removed and a low one set in, but it still had a cantilevered hearth upon which was set a row of logs. A vivid tapestry hung on another wall and in one alcove stood a Queen Anne tallboy. The room had an uncluttered, smart look; yet something about it made Francesca shiver. Then she noticed that Celia was already pouring a drink for Adam and saying in her low seductive tone, 'Darling, your favourite gin and tonic.' As she pressed the glass into his hands, her fingers lingered too long upon his.

To her amazement, Francesca saw Celia turn and get a drink for herself, as though she had again forgotten that she was there. She frowned a little and then caught sight of another table; one which was set for dinner. Silver gleamed, the napkins were immaculate, the centrepiece of coloured grasses tastefully arranged. Something made her look again, and harder this time. The table was distinctly set for two! With a look of alarm Francesca turned to Adam, but his eyes were still focused intently upon his hostess.

Celia was saying, 'You must forgive Giles, darling. He has one of his headaches again. He seems to get them all the time, and you know how he gives in to everything.'

'He's not ill?'

Francesca saw Adam's eyes darken with real concern, and for some reason his voice sounded harder.

'Oh, no! I told him to take a couple of tablets and lie down for ten minutes. He's not ill, but he may well be fast asleep.'

'Then I'll go up.' Adam's voice was gruff now.

'Nonsense! Do sit down, Adam. We must draw some chairs up to the fire.' As she spoke Celia glanced at Francesca again. 'Oh,' she said, frowning a little, 'I really must tell Mrs Coates that you're here, Francesca. I fancy she's prepared something rather special for you. I'm sure you two will get along. I must introduce you to my housekeeper.'

For a moment Francesca felt as though her blood had drained away into the rug beneath her feet. In unspeakable dismay she stared back at Celia, and then at Adam. She could say nothing, she could do nothing, only her slender throat worked painfully.

Adam stood forward and Francesca saw that his face had darkened and that a muscle twitched on one side of his face as though quite out of control. His brows were lowered and he looked angrily at Celia. For one awful moment, Francesca actually thought he might turn and thunder out of the house.

But she was wrong. In agony she saw his expression

change again. Now a playful smile touched his lips and his eyes gleamed brightly below raised brows. 'Then I must have made a terrible mistake, Celia,' he said levelly. 'I distinctly invited Francesca to dine with us.' He took Celia's hand, adding, 'You see, I don't believe she's an ordinary housekeeper. In fact I think we must tread carefully where Miss Lamb is concerned.'

Celia laughed, but Francesca could see that she had lost a little of her composure. She did not quite understand Adam's humour.

'Would you have me changed into some ugly monster?'

'Is she such a witch?' Celia's lips tightened as she flicked a glance at Francesca.

'Mr Greco is merely being kind,' Francesca said, stepping forward now, her finely moulded chin raised, her eyes defiant, although in her heart she was mortified and would have done anything to have been able to run out of the cold house and back over the fells to Thorneyburn Cottage. 'I'd be delighted to meet Mrs Coates,' she told Celia levelly.

With a smile of triumph Celia turned to lead the way.

'Celia!'

Something in Adam Greco's tone made both women start and turn back.

'Celia ...' He came forward and his dark eyes were smiling strangely. He took Celia's hand. 'Celia, you will please apologise to Francesca. You will implore her to sit down with us.'

For a moment Celia paused and then her lips curved into an amused smile. 'You're so gallant, Adam,' she murmured caressingly. 'How can I refuse?' Her gaze moved sensuously over his broad chest and up to the dark skin at his throat. She looked into his eyes. 'I think we could all do with another drink,' she told him with a laugh. 'Come and join the party, Miss Lamb. And do forgive us—it seems that we've made one colossal and unforgivable mistake.'

Francesca could not speak; she started for the door, but Adam caught her arm and drew her back. Because of what she saw in his eyes, a plea not to make things even worse than they were, she swallowed her indignation and forgot about her wounded pride. Then she felt a glass being pressed into her cold hands and heard Adam Greco say in a deep, almost gentle voice, 'For a lady.'

The incident forgotten, at least by Celia, it was now Giles Sutherland's turn to surprise them. In silence they stared at him, for he was still in his dressing gown, unshaven, and very obviously he had been drinking too much.

Was he drunk? Or was he ill? Francesca's first instinct was to go to his aid. When she had known Giles he had drunk very little. Again an uncanny concern for him rose up in Francesca. Giles Sutherland was a most wretched man. She watched him sway up to his wife. 'Those were damn strong aspirin,' he drawled unsteadily. 'It seems our guests are here before I'm dressed.'

'Giles,' Celia said between her teeth, 'please go upstairs. You're making an exhibition of yourself.'

'I'll have a drink and then I'll go.' Giles pursed his pale lips and staring hard into his wife's eyes asserted, 'It's my house, isn't it?'

'I'll go up with you,' said Adam, taking his friend's arm and firmly leading him to the door. 'I'm sure the ladies have things to talk about. They won't miss us for a short time, Giles.'

'I see you've brought Francesca with you.' Giles looked back and smiled pathetically. 'She's a nice girl,' he said. 'But she's not a housekeeper, I can tell you that.'

Francesca took a deep breath of relief as the two men left the room, then she turned to Celia who had been looking very hard at her.

'My husband sounds as though he almost knew you,' she laughed. 'Perhaps he even wishes he did. Giles rather goes for the more fragile type. I think I'll get him a dog. He must want something to look after.' She laughed again, adding with emphasis, 'A lame dog.'

Francesca moved towards the fire. She felt deathly cold. She was thinking of Giles and pitying him more than ever. He was no match for his wife's strong personality. Celia despised him. She had no compassion, no love for him.

'Your husband doesn't look well,' she said, turning back to Celia. 'Perhaps you should telephone the doctor.'

'My dear, I'm not married to an imbecile,' she retorted. 'If Giles feels unwell, then he should see a doctor. I'm not his nursemaid.'

Francesca could not look at Celia now. She shivered again. Celia seemed to exude discontent. Like a cloud it filled the room, like a brooding nemesis.

A little later Adam came heavily back into the room and something in his expression made Francesca start towards him, her blue eyes wide with concern, her lips tightly pursed.

But Adam almost pushed her aside; he strode up to Celia. 'I found this bottle of tablets in his room,' he said

75

in a voice an octave lower than Francesca had ever heard it. 'And they do not happen to be aspirin. Giles took three of them.'

'No wonder he's been sleeping, then,' Celia returned airily, and as she read the label on the bottle: 'They're Mrs Coates's tablets. They're for blood pressure.'

'Then how did they get upstairs?'

'Darling,' Celia's eyebrows arched, 'are you cross-examining me?' she asked Adam. 'You do sound grim. Of course, I'll speak to Mrs Coates. She really mustn't leave such things around.' With an irritable shrug of her shoulders she wandered off, calling peevishly, 'You know, Giles is the limit.' She turned back sharply to them. 'He probably picked them up himself while he was in the kitchen, and took them upstairs. We can't accuse Mrs Coates.'

'We're not accusing anyone,' Adam said slowly, and turning to stare into the fire he added thoughtfully, 'But we must keep an eye on Giles. He gets far too depressed these days. Far too many headaches.'

Now Celia's attitude changed, and coming up behind Adam she asked in a cold voice, 'Did Giles blame me, Adam? Tell me, I want to know. He can be ... odd. You know that.'

Adam put his arm about her shoulders. 'Let's have dinner,' he said gently. 'Everything is all right now. Giles is sleeping, but he may come down later. There's no need for you to get upset.'

'But I am upset, Adam.'

Francesca swallowed hard. Had she not been there she was sure that at that moment Adam would have taken the lovely Celia into his arms. Fortunately the door opened and a stout countrywoman came into the room. She was solemn-eyed, her hair grey and wispy.

Francesca thought there was something familiar about the woman, but she was glad that she could not place her.

'May I bring dinner in now, Mrs Sutherland?' the housekeeper inquired, and for some reason she sounded out of sorts.

'I'd be pleased if you would, Mrs Coates,' Celia returned with the cold tone of authority. 'And while you're here, I'd like to say this. You really must put your blood pressure tablets away safely, Mrs Coates. My husband has just taken some of them in mistake for aspirin.'

'I put them away, Mrs Sutherland,' Mrs Coates asserted in a monotone, 'in the medicine cupboard.' She then glanced at Francesca and inquired in a voice which touched on insolence, 'You did say two for dinner, Mrs Sutherland? I see you've only set places for two.' Her eyes travelled to Francesca again.

'Three, Mrs Coates. Perhaps you would bring another setting. Miss Lamb is joining us.'

'Miss Lamb?' This time Mrs Coates raised her eyebrows as she studied Francesca again. 'The name seems familiar.'

Francesca saw that Mrs Coates was smiling at her and she remembered that smile. Celia's housekeeper was none other than the woman who had been the cook at the village school. At one time she had been a very good friend of her mother's.

Did she recognise her? Would she say anything? With held breath Francesca stared blankly back at the woman.

CHAPTER FOUR

ALTHOUGH it was a bright moonlit night, Adam drove back to Old Beams with stern concentration and he did not speak until they were almost home. The evening had not been a success; the girl at his side sat very still and dispirited.

'I'm sorry about tonight, Francesca,' he said in a gruff voice, as they turned into the drive. 'I'm afraid Celia was a bit out of sorts. Of course, Giles can be a damn fool too.'

'Giles?' Francesca gave him a cold glance. 'I felt sorry for Mr Sutherland,' she said gravely. 'Obviously he was not expected for dinner either.' Her voice shook a little and then her temper rose like a whirlwind and there was nothing she could do. 'Celia had me relegated to the kitchen and her husband to his bed. She'd planned a very cosy tête-à-tête. And you say she was out of sorts!'

'You don't understand, Francesca.' Adam Greco's voice was as stern as his expression. 'How could you?'

'I understand more than you imagine. Remember, the outsider sees all.'

'You don't approve?'

'I most certainly do not!'

'At least Giles has someone to back him up for once,' he said. 'I knew there was some sympathetic communion between the two of you. I noticed it that first night. Giles was so attentive towards you, Francesca, almost protective. Celia noticed it too.'

'I expect you had a laugh together about it?' Francesca's words were forced through tight lips.

'No, I didn't laugh, Francesca. In fact I was rather concerned for you. I'd never seen that light in my friend's eyes before. I'd always taken him for a bit of a cynic. As you've so rightly guessed, Celia and Giles aren't what you call the most happily married couple on earth. But I won't have Celia taking all of the blame. She has her problems.'

'And she has your sympathy,' Francesca put in rather too sharply. 'Don't you think that's rather dangerous?'

'You're a very unworldly girl, Francesca Lamb,' Adam said as he brought the car to a standstill and then sat back to stare pensively at the silver-grey façade of the old house. 'Perhaps that's why I find you so curiously disturbing.' He turned to her now with a smile that was half sad, half mischievous. 'You give me the idea, Francesca, that I might yet be saved.'

Francesca lowered her eyes; she felt as though there was sand in them. Adam Greco was laughing at her now. He was in love with Celia Sutherland, and the fact that she had guessed the truth and disapproved merely amused him. 'I won't thank you for a lovely evening, Mr Greco,' she said abruptly as she thrust open the car door, 'but I will thank you for saving me from the terrible fate of having to eat with Mrs Coates.'

'Francesca!'

He got out of the car and crashed his own door shut. Now he hurried around the front of the car and caught Francesca as she made her way to the entrance. 'Look,' he said, more gently and putting his arm about her shoulder, 'the night is not over yet. Let's have our usual nightcap together, Francesca. Let me play for you.' He drew her closer to him as he steered her into the hall. 'Do you know,' he said, turning her to face him, 'I've come to enjoy this part of the evening, the time I spend with my prim little housekeeper, more perhaps than I would like to admit.'

Francesca said nothing; a feeling of exultation held her; she felt warm and happy again and as they made their way into the sitting room she completely forgot the misery of the evening. She watched Adam take off his coat and then go straight to the piano, and in her heart she knew that music was his salvation. However troubled, he would never seek solace in the arms of a woman. Excitement perhaps, but it was his music that was all-embracing. Celia Sutherland would never rob him of this greater love.

Sitting back in the easy chair by the fire, Francesca closed her eyes. It was amazing, she thought, how a mere man could evoke such sounds, such beauty. Hauntingly sweet notes filled the quiet room and she was still, the pressures of life dormant. She opened her eyes again and watched Adam's hands lightly cover the keyboard. The whole room seemed to be filled with the murmurings of summer. The sunlight was warm on her face, the fragrance of fell flowers in her nostrils. Then the key changed to a more melancholy one and it was autumn. The leaves were crisp and sadly cascading down, slipping away like dreams. The melody changed again and now the abrupt undertones of winter crept into the sound pictures. Francesca thought of her mother now and for a moment it seemed that her mother's spirit was in direct communion with her own. She stood up, her action an involuntary salute to Adam Greco's genius.

The music stopped. Adam stood up too. He stared at Francesca, his dark eyes almost stern and powerful with some kind of preoccupation, then he whispered, 'Are you all right, Francesca?'

'Of course,' she breathed. 'That was wonderful! Almost too wonderful for me.' For a moment she covered her face with her hands. 'Sometimes love and beauty can be too painful.'

'Francesca,' he crossed the room to her and lightly placed his hands upon her shoulders, 'that was indeed a compliment,' he told her gently. He smiled and raised her chin a little with the back of his hand. 'In some uncanny way,' he told her, and his smile changed to a very attractive frown, 'you manage to bring out the best in me.'

'I was carried away,' she whispered, raising her eyes a little. 'Don't laugh at me.'

'Men don't laugh at girls like you, Francesca. They smile, perhaps.'

She looked into his dark eyes now and something within her gave way. She swallowed hard with pent-up emotion and then told him, 'I wish there was something I could do for you. It would seem such a privilege.'

'So you don't disapprove of me entirely?'

She shook her head.

Reaching out to take her hands into his, he said in a low voice, 'I have at least four more weeks work before I start a season of concerts, Francesca. Then it will be really hard work. Promise me you'll stay for at least one winter.'

'I will—I promise.' His music still throbbed in her brain; admiration, worship, made her his prisoner. 'I'll do anything.'

'Good girl!' He continued to stare at her, but he said no more; it was almost as though her words had confused him. The young girl offering her help so sweetly was suddenly almost dear to him. He smiled a little as his feelings were entangled in a mesh of both gratitude and exasperation. This strange girl had so much to offer. She was so different; she was like music herself, young, emotional, sensitive, and as chaste as the dawn. His hand covered his mouth for a moment.

'Would you like some coffee?' Francesca asked, conscious now of the way he was studying her, a little ashamed too of her ridiculous outburst. 'Perhaps it would do you more good than another drink?'

'Would you like some coffee, Francesca?' His smile was charming.

She nodded.

'We'll have some together, then,' he said, and took her arm and steered her out of the room and into the kitchen. 'And I must tell you about my concert. It's next month, and Celia and Giles are hoping to come up to Scotland with me. I'm looking forward to it immensely. I'll be away a couple of nights, perhaps, but if you're nervous I'll arrange for Mrs Noble to sleep in the house.'

'There's no need,' Francesca told him, and she freed herself rather abruptly. 'Please don't bother Mrs Noble. Besides, they're only a few yards away. I'm used to being alone.'

'Why should a girl like you wish to be alone?' He followed her about the kitchen as he spoke. 'You're so unusual, Francesca. You continually amaze me.' He laughed deeply and with the velvety richness that always made her swallow hard. 'I keep expecting to see you turn into some fairy princess. I don't believe you're a housekeeper at all.'

'Then I must leave your service at once, Mr Greco. I wouldn't want to stay here under false pretences.'

'Then I'll believe you.'

'I would,' she bantered. 'Housekeepers are difficult to get.'

'I should say so. Especially out here. They'd have to have a reason for wanting to bury themselves out here.' As he spoke his eyes studied in detail every contour of Francesca's still face. 'They would have to be running away from something. Some terrible grief? Or perhaps some tragic love affair?' His voice faded away, but he continued to stare at Francesca.

Francesca's breath caught in her throat. 'What is it?' she whispered. And because he still continued to stare, 'Is there something wrong?' He was looking at her, but he did not seem to see her; it was as though he looked through her, that he was no longer aware of her presence.

'Mr Greco!'

But Adam Greco could not be withdrawn from the world he now inhabited. It seemed that he neither saw nor heard Francesca, but his arms reached out to her and with all the gentleness in the world he drew her to his breast. Francesca shivered with emotion and some kind of fear, for even as Adam's beautiful hands moved over her she knew that he was locked in some sonorous mood of longing and that she was merely in some strange way a mediator. He was embracing his own talent; the sounds that now filled his head. His hands moved as gently as moonlight through her hair and then with infinite tenderness they dropped 'down to smooth her marble still face. There was no passion, just a dreamlike movement, and as he bent down and his lips met her own, Francesca knew that it was not herself that was important. It was his music! His mind was filled with it, his whole being was elated, joyous, his dark eyes burned with a disturbing light. His thoughts were focused, his fingertips expressed the delight which gladdened his heart.

'You must go and write it all down,' she said softly, catching his hands and drawing back. 'Go into the sitting room now. Do it now. I'll bring your coffee later.'

Just for a moment their gazes met and held in some newborn affinity, then Francesca watched him go purposefully from the room. For a long time after that the house lay perfectly still; as though it too did not dare a breath lest it disturb the genius beneath its roof.

Two hours later, slowly and softly, the old house filled with music again and Adam Greco's orchestral piece was born. As she listened, Francesca's eyes filled with tears. A man of the world, handsome, rich, in all probability immoral. But what did that matter to the world when he could produce such sounds? The world acclaimed him, soon it would revere him. The most sought after women would throw themselves at this idol's feet. He wanted Celia Sutherland and he would have her. Poor Giles was not much of an obstacle. But for one long, heavenly season she herself would at least be close to him, closer than anyone else, and the music which would soon make people rise from their seats and stand spellbound would for a time be as close and warm and as comforting as her own breathing. This was to be her privilege. Perhaps, Francesca mused, one day somebody would even mention her in a book about the world-famous composer Adam Greco.

Listening to him now, moving to the window and watching the wind-maddened clouds race across the sky, baring the moon as they went, leaving the landscape still and stark, she felt herself grow stern. What was the truth behind Adam Greco's worldly façade? she asked herself. Surely he was not an automaton? He must feel all the passion and sadness which his music evoked. Surely this was not the result of technical expertise? He was kind; he had turned her own humiliation into victory that very night, and without offending his Celia. He could be gentle. She lowered her eyelids, remembering his touch. And masterful! She opened her eyes again, remembering the way in which he had swept her up on to White Cloud.

For a while she stood lost in thought, then she crept back to the sitting room. Adam had stopped playing, but he still sat before his piano, head bowed now, his profile melancholy. Francesca moved quietly to his side. 'Congratulations,' she whispered. He did not answer her and seemed to be still lost in a remote world of his own. 'I'm going to bed now, Mr Greco. It's after one o'clock.'

At this he got to his feet. His dark eyes glinted. He was frowning a little at the girl who stood before him as solemn as a child. 'Then we're both going in the same direction,' he teased, and the smile was about his lips again. 'May I escort you?'

'I don't need an escort, Mr Greco,' she told him as she turned quickly away. 'Goodnight,' she said. She was trembling for no reason at all, wondering now which Adam Greco she preferred. The smiling, worldly Adam, or the one who could drop her a light kiss as a courteous salute? Or perhaps the Adam Greco who could caress her without even realising that she was there?

'Goodnight, Miss Lamb.'

The use of her surname made Francesca glance back. But Adam was contemplating his piano again, his thoughts far away. She stood still for a moment, then she whispered, 'Adam, I think you should go to bed. There's always tomorrow.'

He began to play a little, accompanying his words,

'So you don't like Miss Lamb?' A little cascade of notes. 'I don't like it either. Francesca is a sweet name, like an endearment.' His fingers ran lightly over the keys again. 'Goodnight, Francesca,' he murmured. 'Goodnight.'

'Goodnight, Adam,' she whispered. 'Goodnight.'

'Just one moment.'

Francesca had reached the door. He swung around on his piano stool, claimed her gaze.

Francesca swallowed with embarrassment because of its powerful concentration. 'Yes?' she whispered.

'Let's forget about the Greco too,' he said, and his voice was strangely authoritative. 'I like the way you say Adam.'

Francesca smiled and slipped away out of the room. She felt happy, almost too happy. And just a little afraid.

Next morning Adam had little to say at breakfast and Francesca watched him go off for his usual canter on White Cloud with a deepening conviction that he was going to a secret rendezvous with Celia Sutherland. A black fog spread over her heightened spirits and she felt lonely again, almost to the point of desolation. Then she thought about Giles and without thinking she hurried off to the telephone with the intention of ringing Thorneyburn House and inquiring after him. But just in time reality caught up with her. She was housekeeper at Old Beams and no longer a friend of the Sutherlands. She was not in a position to ring Giles. With a sigh she turned back to her kitchen. She went to the dresser, opened the drawer and once again took out her mother's old recipe book. She held it tightly between her cold fingers, trying desperately to gain some comfort from it, closing her eyes, trying to imagine that her mother was there again. 'Now come along, Francesca,' she could hear her mother saying. 'There's no time for moping. The sun is high and bright, the world is beautiful, so don't waste a minute.'

Francesca put the book back in the drawer and shut it. Her mother had been a brave woman and she had talked sense. She would have a walk, go down to the village. She remembered Kirklaw quite well. Once or twice she had gone down to the church with her mother. She would go again, but this time on a pilgrimage to her mother's grave. Bracing herself, Francesca decided that it was a suitable morning for such an act.

After a chat with Mrs Noble about dinner and a few other domestic matters, she walked off down the drive, pausing only to speak to Mr Noble, who extended an open invitation to her to watch their colour television whenever she felt like it. The elderly man's shy overture made Francesca feel better and she tightened the belt of her emerald corduroy jacket and started down over the fields towards the village which lay in a hollow with only the church spire to draw attention to the fact that it was there. It was two miles away and it took Francesca half an hour to reach the small row of cottages, the post-office and church. The school was empty now, its windows sad and grey, its pupils only the grazing goats about the closed door. There was no one in sight and everything was silent.

Francesca stood for a moment gazing over the silver and lime lichened wall, thinking of how the old church was like both a womb and a tomb. She pushed open the white wooden gate and made her way slowly up the paved path, pausing now and again to view the more impressive sepulchres. Then she came to a standstill and as she stared down at the small headstone of her mother's grave a rush of suffocating sorrow brought her to her knees. 'In memory of Alicia Lamb ...' she read, and that was all.

For some time she knelt on the cold turf, memories blanching her stiff face, her tears too frozen to fall. Then, caressingly, the sun's warm rays spread through the old beech trees and looking up she knew that she must smile too. 'For heaven's sake, Francesca,' she heard her mother chide, 'I can't bear your face when it's so long. Pretend you're happy, Francesca, and you will be.'

Francesca stood up and at that moment she knew that her grieving days were over. She could now face up to reality. Her mother was dead, but some of her spirit lived on in her own heart. With a feeling akin to joy she turned and walked lightly away.

The sun was high and Francesca decided to take the short cut back through the woods. There, where she had played as a child, she joined in the whirling, twirling dance of the autumn leaves. She danced and gave expression to her own new feeling of freedom and release. She even called out as she had done as a child, then listening to the resounding echo of her own voice. She jumped up and reached for a branch, swung with delight. The sunlight streamed through the tall trees and burnished her long hair, the crisp air whipped the colour into her cheeks and polished her bright blue eyes. Then she fell back, exhausted, against the great ribbed bole of a tree. She closed her eyes. She felt so crazily happy that she shouted out, loud and long, 'Adam Greco! Adam Greco!'

Dropping down from the old Wanny line, Francesca made her way across the fields and then up on to the country lane again. She had gone about a hundred yards when a car pulled up beside her and looking around she saw to her surprise that it was Giles Sutherland.

'Hello, Francesca,' he called, and thrust open the car door. 'Come on, jump in. I'll give you a lift.'

Francesca sank on to the seat beside him.

'You look like a sunbeam this morning,' he told her, giving her a half sad, half admiring glance.

'How are you?' she asked, feeling just a little sobered. 'I must say I was worried about you last night.'

'If I thought you were really concerned, Francesca,' he said levelly as they drove on, 'I'd be a happy man.'

'You should be more careful about taking tablets. You just don't swallow anything, Giles.'

'Giles?' He stopped the car and turned to her. 'Do you know,' he said, and his eyes were very grave, 'it's wonderful to hear you calling me Giles again, Francesca.'

'Habit, I suppose. I still think of you as Giles.' She looked at him, a little impatiently now. 'Please don't stop here,' she said swiftly. 'I must get back.'

'And I must apologise,' Giles said as he turned to face Francesca. 'I fully intended to be there to protect you from Celia last night. I know her so well. I knew she'd be up to something. Mrs Coates told me what happened.'

'I see.' Carefully Francesca inquired, 'I thought at first that I remembered Mrs Coates, but I must have been mistaken. She would have remembered me.'

'I don't suppose she did. You've changed, Francesca. You're not a little schoolgirl now. I just wish you were.' Giles turned to stare pensively out of the window for a moment. 'I wish we could turn back the clock.'

Francesca straightened up. 'Giles,' she said smartly, 'will you please drive me back to Old Beams. I have work to do. And you must make the most of your life. You're a most fortunate man. You have wealth and a stunning-looking wife. What more do you want?'

'You know what I want, Francesca.' He turned to her, his voice choking in his throat. 'I want you. I've always wanted you.'

Something in his tone made Francesca swallow painfully. There was something almost pathetic about Giles. She felt sorry for him, so sorry that she did not realise that his hand had slipped about her shoulder.

Suddenly he was close and she was looking into his pale face, his stricken eyes. 'Francesca,' he breathed, and his words were full of entreaty, 'Francesca, forgive me. I don't know why I was such a fool. But I can make it up to you. I can protect you. I'm rich.'

Francesca sat back stiffly against the car door. 'You can do nothing for me, Mr Sutherland,' she said coldly. 'You decided that a few years ago. Celia is your problem, not me. Besides, I don't need anyone to look after me.'

'But I can't forget you.' Giles grabbed out at her now. Desperately he clung to her. 'Francesca, be my friend, just my friend. If we can just meet and talk. I'll be good to you.'

Flushed with annoyance, Francesca struggled free. 'If your marriage is such a failure,' she flung at him, 'why don't you get a divorce? Why insult me?'

At last Giles sank back, his thin cheeks hollow now, his expression grim. 'The Sinclair and Sutherland marriage was a business merger,' he told her in a monotone. 'That marriage is still on. Celia has no intention of swopping me for a poor man.' He laughed cynically. 'She couldn't love a cat, but when the right time comes she'll find a way to liberate herself. As she so rightly says, wealth is the only true liberator.'

'I am sorry, Giles,' Francesca said more softly, thinking of Adam Greco and the money he must eventually make. 'But please, I must go. I'm a working girl.'

With a forced smile, Giles turned to look into her troubled eyes. 'Don't worry,' he said knowingly, 'I'll make sure that Adam doesn't work you too hard. I can at least do that.'

'Please, Giles . . .'

'Just one kiss, Francesca, for old times' sake.'

There was no escape. Roughly she was drawn into his arms.

'I can't go on remembering, longing, wishing,' he murmured despairingly against her cheek. Then his full lips were hard against hers and she sank back as he pressed against her, hating his kiss, hating the fierce hunger of his body, loathing the way in which he strove to part her lips with his own.

He pushed her away abruptly. 'All right,' he said, and now his tone held a hint of menace, 'I'll take you back. In any case, this isn't exactly the place to kiss a girl, is it?'

They drove in a bitter silence and when they reached the house they saw Adam standing chatting to Mr Noble. He waved to them and then followed the car up to the forecourt. Giles got out. 'Hello there, Adam,' he called, struggling to sound like himself again. 'I'm sorry about last night.'

'You certainly gave us all a shock, Giles.' Adam studied his friend intently for a few moments, then he turned to Francesca, who had got out of the car and was hurrying into the house.

'She's a nice girl,' Giles remarked, following his friend's gaze. 'Where did you find her, Adam?'

Adam's shoulders lifted. He smiled and told Giles, 'I didn't. I think Francesca found me.'

Giles walked behind him, but now a dull flush brought his pale face to life and the light of a new conviction brightened his eyes feverishly. 'I came over to talk about the concert,' he said smartly. 'Celia wants to know where we'll be staying. That is, if we can't get back the same night.'

'There'll be a party at the Swan Hotel after the concert,' Adam told his friend, and he turned to wait for him to catch up. 'We could stay there if necessary. I'll certainly give them a ring.'

'Good.' Giles walked a little ahead now. 'Are you working this morning, Adam?' he asked, and by his tone there was plainly something on his mind. 'I'd like to talk.'

'I'm sorry, Giles, but I must work this morning. It's imperative. There's something I must get down. It's in my mind. I must see to it at once or I may well lose it for ever.' He strode up and laid his hand on his friend's shoulder. 'What about coming over tonight?' he suggested with a more encouraging smile. 'Let's have a quiet drink together.'

They walked on into the house and then into the dining-room. Francesca, coming downstairs, saw them and pausing, she wondered if she should offer them coffee. Then she heard Adam say, 'Yes, come over and have a drink with me, Giles. Or rather with us. Francesca and I usually have a nightcap together.' He laughed a little, adding, 'I'm not quite so lonesome as I used to be.'

Giles was laughing low in his throat now and something made Francesca stay still.

'You needn't laugh like that,' Adam tossed back.

'Francesca Lamb is a very nice girl, and an extremely efficient housekeeper. Also she's not the kind of girl you easily rob of her will power. She has a mind of her own, and a very charming mind too.'

'Very moral, you mean?' Giles smirked.

'Certainly very trusting.' This time Adam laughed.

Francesca turned white and gripped the banister-rail. The voices had receded a little, but she could still hear Giles. He was tauntingly playful and saying, 'And I suppose you would be the last man to corrupt such a girl?'

'If you mean would I make love to the girl, then no.' Adam laughed, but strangely now. 'How do you make love to a girl like that?' he asked, and his voice was very sober now. 'Can you tell me that, Giles?'

'She's not unpleasant to look at,' Giles suggested warily.

'If you like that particular kind of freshness,' Adam Greco went on, crossing the room to a small cabinet where he thoughtfully set about pouring out two drinks. 'And if you can stand that awesome honesty in her eyes, that directness.'

'You sound a little afraid of her.'

'We're all afraid of the innocent.'

Francesca crept away to the kitchen where with fumbling fingers she set about filling a vase with flowers. They were talking about her as though she were some different species, almost as though they imagined they could do as they pleased with her. 'If you like that particular kind of freshness ... that awesome honesty in her eyes.' How could she ever look at Adam Greco again? How could she bear loving such a man? For she was in love with him; she knew that. She had been so happy; she had felt so lighthearted, so free from sorrow. That morning she had felt young again. With a gesture of frustration and bitterness, she stuck another flower into the vase. Tears were pricking her eyes. She was suddenly sick of being alone, of being nobody, of pretending, for in the woods that morning hadn't she imagined herself to be a princess waiting for her prince? Hadn't she called out, 'Adam Greco! ... Adam Greco!'?

There would be no more nightcaps for her. She would close her heart to his music, his talent, his brilliance. Tonight she would accept Mr Noble's kind offer and watch television with them. She would, in future, keep her place and as her mother had told her, keep her privacy and self-respect. Wisdom had come a little late, but she knew now just how to conduct herself.

With these thoughts in mind, Francesca busied herself all day. She made the evening meal and after setting the table in the dining-room she hurriedly went upstairs to change. Adam met her in the hall just as he came out of the sitting room where he had been working all day. He looked flushed and excited, but his eyes shadowed a little the moment he saw Francesca. 'Are you going somewhere?' he asked, his eyes hard on her tunic jacket.

'The Nobles have kindly invited me to watch their colour television,' she told him quickly, avoiding the disappointment which registered in his eyes. 'Everything is ready for you, Mr Greco. I hope you enjoy your meal.'

With a frown on his face he followed her to the door. 'Do you prefer colour television?' he asked rather abruptly. 'If so, I can soon have one installed.'

She did not answer, so he asked, 'Will you be late?'

'I don't know. Does it matter?'

'No, of course not. Do as you please.'

He watched her go; the long fluid line of her neck, the smooth, swaying brown hair, the slim, erect back, then slowly, his hands deep in his pockets, he went back to his own lonely table. The dinner looked delicious, but he had no appetite. As he stared down at the small vase, the carefully arranged centrepiece, a new kind of tenderness and gratitude for the lovely young girl who had come to housekeep for him flooded through his veins. Restlessly he strode about. But there was no music in his soul now; only a grey anxiety. Was she suddenly dissatisfied? Had the incident at Thorney-burn House upset her more than he had imagined? He thought of Celia, and now he suddenly laughed. He was hungry again. Celia, he contemplated cynically, would make any man hungry.

Giles came over at nine o'clock. Again Adam's dark eyes registered disappointment. 'You're alone, then?' he said. 'Didn't Celia want to come over?'

'I didn't ask her.'

'I see.'

'Aren't you going to offer me a drink?' said Giles. 'You look a thousand miles away, Adam. I hope I haven't arrived at one of your inspired moments?'

'No,' Adam replied thoughtfully, 'the bird has flown.' Then, forcing a smile, he pushed a chair forward and said, 'Sit down, Giles. For some odd reason I feel like getting drunk.'

Giles considered his friend from below lidded eyes. 'You usually have a good gallop, Adam—I mean, when you want to get something out of your system. It must be something very special this time. Is your work worrying you?'

'No, no,' Adam's answer seemed to come from a

hundred miles away. 'What can I get you to drink? The same as usual?'

In the Nobles' cottage Francesca tried to rouse some enthusiasm for their new television set. But the harder she tried to keep her mind on the programme the more determined Adam Greco was to steal back into it.

'You look pale, dearie. Are you all right?' Mrs Noble asked in a kindly tone. 'You work far too hard, you know. Thomas was just saying so this morning. When you're not working you're running about the fells like a wild thing. It doesn't seem natural for a girl of your age. You should have friends of your own age.'

Francesca forced a smile. The Nobles were doing their best to please her. She thanked them again and said how nice their cottage was and how she admired their taste. All the same, she was thankful when she was making her way back to the house. It was ten o'clock and she wanted to go to bed. She hurried by Giles Sutherland's car and then quickly and silently made her way upstairs to her room. It had been a strange day; she felt as though she had been resurrected only to be buried again.

Once in bed, she pulled the covers up over her head, as though in an effort to hide herself from the hard world about her. She was in love with Adam Greco, but had she really imagined that he might love her? A man in his position was not likely to fall in love with a fresh-faced, honest-eyed girl who took the drudgery out of life for him.

She could not sleep. She lay awake now in the moon-lit room thinking of the time when she had slept in a much smaller house and been so much more happy. She thought of her mother, with sadness but no grief.

It was almost as though her mother forbade her to grieve. She lay very still in the large bed until she heard the clock in the hall solemnly strike twelve. Then a car started up and she knew that Giles was leaving. She watched the car beams spread over the wall of the bedroom, then she lay perfectly still again, wondering if Adam might play as he usually did before he retired for the night. But no sound came and the house seemed uncannily still.

Francesca closed her eyes, but only to struggle against another agonising rush of thought. She would never sleep that night, she told herself. She refused to lie there tormenting herself, going over and over the humiliating things which had been said about her. She would go downstairs and make herself a warm drink. Never had she felt so wound up, so tense, so miserably frustrated.

But there was no time; at that moment she heard Adam's footsteps on the landing. She caught her breath, deciding to wait until he was in his room before she ventured downstairs. But the footsteps had stopped. Her heart beat very fast now and she held her breath. The door was slowly opening.

Adam stood there, the moonlight on his handsome face, a face taut now with some inward struggle. 'So you are awake?' he said. 'I thought you would be.'

As he came forward Francesca drew the sheet up a little higher. 'What do you want?' she asked him in a breathless voice. 'Why didn't you knock at the door?'

He stood perfectly still at the foot of her bed, aware of her shock, aware too of an excitement, a strange still excitement between them.

'What do you want?' she said again, and this time her voice shook.

He moved to the side of her bed now and sitting down gently on the edge of it he took the hem of the sheet from her shaking hands. 'I want you to come downstairs,' he told her in a firm, strong voice. 'You can drink as much as you wish. You can kick my table and smash up my dishes.' He paused to frown and then smile critically into her shocked eyes. 'Do what you must, Francesca, but please take that look of outrage from your eyes.'

'Would you prefer me to look boringly honest all the time?' she burst out, giving herself away before she could stop herself.

Now Adam Greco stood up. For a moment his countenance was dark, stern. Then he sighed and frowning down at her he said carefully, 'You must know that an eavesdropper never hears any good of himself. You said you were a mature woman, Francesca . . .?'

'I am a woman.'

He smiled and closed his eyes for a moment, for again she held up the sheet which denied him the evidence. 'Come downstairs,' he said gently, and as his gaze focused upon her smooth bare shoulders, 'There's still time for us to have our nightcap together.' And turning to stride slowly from the room he called back, 'Whatever you've deduced from an overheard conversation, Francesca, I missed you tonight.'

'I'll come down,' she whispered. 'I won't be long.'

He paused at the door and glanced back at her. 'Wrap up,' he said gently and just as he would have addressed a child. 'It's chilly down there.'

CHAPTER FIVE

THE following hour held for Francesca moments of enchantment she was destined to add to her list of precious memories. For a while they sat by the fire, enjoying their drinks, Adam talking softly of his coming concert season; of its heavy demands and happier attractions. He lit a cigar and then a warm congenial silence followed. It seemed to Francesca that a calm had settled over the old house.

Adam got up and moved over to the piano and Francesca smiled, wrapped her dressing-gown more snugly about herself, then sank back into the comforting luxury of her chair. She closed her eyes.

This time Adam's playing brought a strange ache to her heart. He played his new composition and each poignant note seemed to hold some message of joy, each cadence filled her being with a spreading happiness, a stream of fresh hope. The music was indescribably beautiful. It seemed to open the door to another world, a world of peace and truth, of love and wonder. Adam Greco was a privileged man and through these portals, Francesca knew he walked alone. He was no longer with her; his spirit had moved away. Suddenly she felt lonely, conscious of a vacuum within herself that made her bow her head and swallow with emotion.

Ten minutes later, Francesca opened her eyes again. Adam had stopped playing and the room was very still, the only sound, the crackling of the fire.

'Francesca?'

She raised her eyes to his.

'You have forgiven me? We're friends once again, I hope?' He smiled and half turned to lay his palms lightly on the keys. 'You accept my apology?'

Francesca understood; his playing had been his offering. She nodded, but still she could not speak. Never had she felt so moved, so touched.

He got up and crossed to her, stood staring down at her, half smiling, half frowning. 'You were offended because you heard me say I had no intention of making love to you?'

Francesca frowned now and averted her eyes.

'Does that mean you would prefer it if I did?'

He was surely teasing her? Still she could not look at him but she said levelly, 'Why should I want you to make love to me, Mr Greco? You don't love me and I'm afraid I'm an old-fashioned girl. If you must know . . .'

'Mr Greco,' he put in teasingly, smiling now at the girl who sat so primly, so charmingly proper.

'I'd like to tell you,' Francesca raced on, 'that I still believe that to love and marry a person for ever and ever must be a very precious thing.'

'Who would disagree?'

The tone of his voice made her look up this time and she saw that he was laughing. But with great charm he took her hands into his own and told her gently, 'You know, I did miss you tonight, Francesca. I just had to bring you down. I want you to understand, more than anyone else I want you to understand my music.'

It was a great compliment and at once it was pressed within the folds of Francesca's brain for ever. She did understand his music; while he played she had some kind of affinity with his soul, she knew that. And because he knew it too, she felt calmed and almost happy.

Even the thought of Celia no longer tormented her. Withdrawing her hands, she once again pledged herself to work for Adam Greco's good, and to ask no more.

For the following week the house was filled with great music and great silences. Francesca worked hard too. She knew that Adam was tensing up and she excused his moments of irritability and abruptness. An artist had to tense up, he told her, or his work was worth nothing.

The day before they were to travel to Scotland, Giles came over to Old Beams and Francesca hurried away to make coffee for the two men whom she had left chatting in the sitting room. Then to her surprise she heard another car drive up and almost immediately Celia's shrill excited voice echoed through the house. She took the coffee through to them, smiled briefly at Celia, who looked even more stunning than usual in a cream suede tunic suit and bronze-coloured sweater, then returned to the kitchen. But she had noticed the bright seduction in Celia's eyes and again she stood for a few moments, hugging herself, conscious of a sense of doom. She was being silly, she told herself. What harm could a woman like Celia do Adam Greco? He was a genius but he was also a man. At such a time he would have little energy left for Celia. It would take all his concentration to get through the concert. Hadn't he told her of the great demands the season made upon him? Busying herself again, Francesca strove to keep calm. How could she protect such a man? she asked herself, and for the first time she even smiled at her own foolishness.

'Oh, there you are! Always at your sink.'

Francesca pulled herself together as Giles strode into the room. 'Hello,' she said levelly, 'what are you doing here?'

'I've come to see you, Francesca. Is there any reason why I shouldn't?'

'I thought you'd come to see Adam.'

'I had, but it seems that my wife has now taken over.'

'Adam hasn't much time,' Francesca returned with a hint of aggression.

'He always has time for Celia,' Giles said. 'You must have noticed that.'

Francesca turned to the dresser. Her heart was racing, angrily. She wished Giles would go; she did not want to talk to him.

'I've been thinking things over,' he said, and came and stood at her side. 'Giving you a little time to adjust. Francesca, I did rather rush you. I'm sorry about that. Have you missed me at all?'

'Of course I haven't,' Francesca told him. 'I'm a working woman, Giles. I have no time for daydreams.'

He raised his eyebrows. 'I'd been hoping that Adam would invite you to come along to Scotland with us.'

'Why should he do that?' Francesca returned sharply. 'I'm his housekeeper, not his nurse.' She pursed her lips and looked into his eyes. 'Please don't start all that nonsense again, Giles. I have enough to contend with at the moment.'

'Oh! I hope Adam isn't giving you too much trouble.' He grinned and moved away as he added, 'He likes the ladies, but I expect you've already found that out.'

'Then perhaps it's just as well that I'm not one,' Francesca shot with some of the old bitterness. 'And please, Giles, don't come to my kitchen to hide. Why don't you go and assert yourself for once? Why do you allow Celia to make a fool of you?'

'Does she make a fool of me?' Giles turned to look at her now and his eyes were vaguely sad. 'Is that what you think?'

'I do. But then it doesn't matter what I think.'

'I can see you'll never forgive me, Francesca.'

'I can never forget, Giles,' she told him. 'But it no longer hurts. There's nothing so dead as a dead infatuation.'

'You never loved me, then?'

Francesca bit her lip; it was against her nature to hurt anyone. 'If I did, I'm certainly over it,' she told him with a forced laugh. 'The spots have all gone.'

Giles walked around her now, a sly little smile hovering about his lips. 'Perhaps you're even in love with someone else, Francesca?' He paused and his eyes grew hard again. 'I only hope you're not stupid enough to get ideas about Adam. He has so much to give the world, therefore he takes what he pleases in return. I'm afraid where women are concerned he's not what you would call moral.'

'I'm not interested in Adam Greco's morals,' Francesca returned hotly and with a sensation of not being able to get her breath. 'You certainly get some funny ideas, Giles. But let me tell you this: I'm happy in my position here. I'm neither interested in your marriage nor Adam Greco's morals. My purpose in life at this moment is to save enough money to buy Thorneyburn Cottage.' She turned back to the window and now her blue eyes grew misty and her voice dropped to a whisper as she told him, 'I want to go home, Giles, I want to go back. Perhaps even you can understand that.'

'Francesca ...' Giles's voice had changed now and he stood frowning at the floor. 'Francesca,' he began again, 'you sound so sad. A girl as young as you are shouldn't be sad. In a way I understand, but why look backwards?'

She turned on him now, her face flushed with emotion. 'Because I know where I was most happy,' she told him with a burst of confidence. 'I loved that simple life, Giles. My mother was happy, and I want to be like my mother.'

'But your mother was a widow.' Giles looked alarmed now. 'You don't want to be alone, Francesca.'

'My mother was never alone. I can see that you don't understand, Giles.'

'Perhaps not.' He watched her turn back to her work. 'But I could help. Yes, I could help you to get Thorneyburn Cottage back. It would be quite simple, and I think it's a good idea.'

'You would help me?' Francesca moistened her lips as she faced him again. Something she read in his eyes made her straighten up and say, 'I mean to pay every penny myself, Giles. How much do you imagine the place would cost? Could you give me some idea?'

'Francesca!' In a moment he had taken her roughly into his arms. His eyes were feverishly bright now, his lips trembling as he muttered, 'Don't you understand, you can have the place. I can give it to you. There's no need for you to work for every penny, you silly girl.'

Desperately, Francesca struggled to free herself. 'In return for what?' she demanded, glaring at him, her breath coming in angry little spurts. 'Perhaps you would have me pay a greater price?'

Giles's face was very grave as his arms slid to his sides again. 'In return for a smile, Francesca,' he said in a constrained voice. 'Just a smile. I want to see you again as the girl you used to be, the girl who used to laugh. I haven't seen that dimple for a long time, Francesca. I can't be responsible for this. Don't you understand? I'm suffering too.'

'You have a wife, Giles, a fine house. You may have children.'

'Children?'

Something in his sneering tone made Francesca look up at him in dismay. 'What's wrong with having children?' she asked sharply. 'You used to like children, Giles.'

'Celia doesn't. She refuses to discuss the matter. She doesn't want any children. She's told me that she'll never have a child of mine.'

For once Giles's voice was strong with anger and humiliation and Francesca heard herself whisper sincerely, 'I'm sorry, Giles. I'm sorry about that.'

'Don't be.' His voice was gratingly harsh. 'Don't waste your pity, Francesca. Sometimes I think Celia and I deserve each other.'

Francesca's gentleness overcame her disgust. 'Give her time,' she told him with a forced laugh. 'It seems to take us all so long to decide what we really want.'

After studying her for a few moments Giles asked, 'What are you going to do while we're all away?'

'My work, of course,' she answered lightly. 'The house will still be here.'

'I see.'

He continued to stare at her, so that Francesca at last broke away to busy herself noisily about the room. 'I really mustn't waste any more time,' she told him, as she brought reality back into the room with a clatter of pans. 'You'd better go, Giles. They'll wonder what you're doing.'

The moment Giles went, she went to the dresser and opening the drawer she again took out her mother's old recipe book. It was an involuntary action, and holding the little book brought her comfort. She no longer grieved for that which could not be, but there was still a sadness in her heart. At times the world looked decidedly grey. Then she heard some activity in the hall and raised voices. The Sutherlands were going.

A few minutes later Adam strode into the kitchen. He looked very pleased and he said confidently, 'We're leaving on Wednesday, Francesca. I have one or two rehearsals. Of course, I'll ring you. I'm sure you'll want to know how I get on.' Smiling now, he added, 'After all your patience, you deserve to. You'll watch the concert on television, of course.'

'I'll look for you in the crowd.' Francesca tried to sound teasing and lighthearted. 'And of course I'll send good vibrations. Are you playing your new composition?'

'Yes, I am.' Adam paused to consider her with frowning concentration. 'Francesca, you must listen. You won't let anything stop you, will you?'

She shook her head vigorously, then she asked, 'How long will you be away, Mr Greco?'

'I don't really know,' he told her as he turned to frown about the room. 'Celia wants to do some shopping in Edinburgh, so she may travel up with me. Giles is just coming for the concert.'

'Doesn't her husband enjoy shopping?' Francesca inquired archly. 'I don't suppose you'll have any time for window-gazing?'

'You're quite right.' He grinned rather foolishly and in an attractive gesture frowned knowingly at her. 'But then I can't leave Celia absolutely marooned.'

'I can't imagine a woman like Mrs Sutherland being

marooned,' Francesca said lightly. 'Someone, I'm sure, would go to her rescue.'

'I dare say.' Adam laughed softly to himself and for a moment or two his gaze rested lightly upon the slim, erect back which for some reason had been turned to him. Then he left the room and a few minutes later the old house stirred once again to the sound of music.

Francesca stood very still, her gaze lowered. Incredibly beautiful sounds filtered into every corner of her heart and brain. Adam Greco's music was achingly beautiful; it stirred her soul, her skin. She loved his music! She loved him! Watching him go off to Scotland with another man's wife she would still love him. It seemed that she was destined to love and lose.

'Darling, are you sure you've got your fur jacket? There's a decided nip in the air.'

Francesca had listened to Celia and Adam laughingly checking up before they had left together for Edinburgh. Old Beams was now like a school without a master, a church without a priest. Francesca herself felt the gladness going out of her. Anxiety now laid siege upon her; she moved about the house stiffly, a far-away expression on her face, her eyelids heavy. She tried desperately hard not to think of Celia Sutherland, but the vision of Celia laughing provocatively up into Adam's face was ever there to torment her. She talked to the Nobles, watched their television and even had a meal with them. Then she set about the task of getting the house ready for the virtuoso's triumphant return. She would fill the house with autumn leaves, she told herself in a fit of enthusiasm, make it golden and glorious for the return of a man whose gift brought pleasure to thousands. She would do her utmost to make his homecoming memorable.

But how could she stop thinking of Celia? How could she stop reminding herself that Adam and Celia were spending a few days together, staying at the same hotel? Again jealousy rose up to lash her with images of Adam making love to the most desirable Celia, a woman who only cared about herself, money and fame.

By Monday Francesca had grown quite sullen. She almost feared Adam's return now. What would she read in his eyes? In Celia's? Did he really merely accept Celia and other women as part of his success, his right?

Her silence and withdrawal worried Mrs Noble. 'If you're nervous in the house, why don't you come over and sleep in the cottage?' she asked, and her handsome face puckered with concern for the young girl she had come to admire. 'There's no need for you to be all alone. Besides, it's not right. Mr Greco expects too much of you. Thomas says he's taking advantage, and this time I'm inclined to agree.'

Francesca was not listening. She was thinking of Giles. He was to drive up to Scotland that day. In all probability he would be there now, just in time to make everything look respectable. But it was Monday night, and Adam had told her that he might travel back straight after the concert. There would be drinks, of course, but he had said that did not take long. If he did travel all the way back that night he would surely be hungry? Francesca gave a little smile of triumph now, and with the determined air of a housekeeper she made her way to the kitchen. She would make something very special and put it away in the hostess trolley. Mr Noble would set the fire in the sitting room. Everything was to be ready for Adam's homecoming. Even if he came in the early hours of the morning everything he wanted would be there for him.

Francesca worked hard all morning preparing suitable dishes for a late meal and after lunch she went for a walk over the fields. She loved tripping along over the springy northern moss; she loved the woods where the beech and birch trees rose like golden fountains. She loved to hear the little twigs and the fir cones squeak and crack beneath her feet. With armfuls of leaves she returned to the house and by six o'clock everything was in order; Francesca sighed with satisfaction and went upstairs to get ready for the concert which she was to watch in the privacy of the sitting room. Afraid of showing some kind of emotion, she had declined the Nobles' offer to watch their television this time.

The room had not yet warmed up, so she kept on her grey and green check tunic suit, deciding that she would change later, certainly before Adam arrived back. That was if he came. Francesca supposed that he would come. With Giles in Edinburgh, there would be nothing for Adam to stay for, she thought with a rush of bitterness. But again she calmed herself, and by seven o'clock she was all agog and sitting before the television waiting for the programme to be announced.

She caught her breath. The curtains swept back from the screen. The stage was set. A great roar rose from the audience. The conductor, an elderly man with a pleasant smile, walked on to the stage, bowed to the audience, bowed to his fellow musicians. There were one or two introductions, a short speech, and then Adam Greco was being announced. Another roar from the audience filled the hall, then there was complete silence.

Francesca felt as though her heart had missed a beat

as she watched Adam come into full focus. He looked so breathtakingly handsome, so dark, so beautiful. Tears rushed to her eyes, her throat felt full. She smiled because it seemed that Adam smiled right at her. He bowed courteously and the house again applauded him. There were lots of young people; people in clothes as gay as Adam's black, hip-fitting toreador trousers and unconventional yellow silk shirt with its frilled jabot and fabulous sleeves. Just as his range of music was wide, he had established a wide range of age groups in his audience. They loved him; they applauded him again.

The house grew still and expectant. Adam was now seated before his piano. The conductor's baton was raised. Francesca sank back as the first movement of Adam's new concerto filled the great hall. He was like some dark prince, debonair, brilliant, fantastically gifted. Now a delicious shudder rippled up Francesca's spine, the fine hair on the nape of her neck stirred; enthralled by the music, she closed her eyes. Adam Greco's music evoked in her imagination everything that was most beautiful.

Her dreams were cut short by the sound of the telephone and with a frown of annoyance she got up quickly and ran out into the hall. Anxious to get back as quickly as possible, she grabbed up the receiver. 'Hello,' she said sharply.

'Francesca?'

Francesca turned white. Giles? But he was in Edinburgh! 'Giles?' she whispered breathlessly. 'What do you want? Where are you? Why aren't you listening to Adam?'

'Francesca, will you come over?'

'Over where?' Francesca felt herself go weak with

shock. 'Giles,' she cried suddenly and with emotion she could not control, 'aren't you in Edinburgh?'

'Of course I'm not in Edinburgh! I'm at home. I'm in bed. I'm ill.'

He sounded distraught. For a moment Francesca could not answer.

'Francesca? Are you still there?'

'Yes.' The word was like a dry stick in her throat.

'Francesca, will you come over to Thorneyburn House? Please, I feel so awful.' His voice was bleak now.

Angrily she burst out, 'I'm listening to Adam. I can't come now. Why don't you get in touch with Celia? Or better still, get Mrs Coates to call your doctor. I can't do anything for you, Giles.'

'I don't want you to do anything. I just don't want to be alone. Celia's at the concert and Mrs Coates is on her long week-end off.'

He was panting, breathless.

'Have you a temperature?' she asked, concern shadowing her face now. 'You sound breathless.'

'I feel dreadful, Francesca. Just this once, do me this favour. I feel as though I must talk to someone. I feel . . .'

'All right, Giles. I'll come over.' The quick decision brought a pained look to Francesca's eyes. The last thing she wanted to do was to visit Thorneyburn House with everyone away except Giles. But he did sound ill. She felt compelled to go. As soon as she got there she would telephone his doctor, leave as quickly as she could.

'Francesca?'

'Don't bother to talk,' she called back, breathless herself now. 'Just lie still, Giles. You are in bed?'

This time he did not answer and panicking a little, Francesca threw down the receiver and ran back to the sitting room. For a moment her gaze dwelt upon Adam, then she turned and hurried back into the hall for her coat. Confused, she went back again. It was the second movement of his new composition. He looked pale, she thought, his glossy black hair tangled a little over his perspiring brow. His eyes were half closed, his black lashes sheltering the emotion Francesca knew must be reflected in his eyes. His mouth was gentle, the lips which had gently caressed her own curved expressively.

She had to go. With a little groan of disappointment she tore herself away.

Adam had left his car and she was very soon on her way to Thorneyburn House. She would stay until the doctor arrived and then get back to Old Beams as quickly as possible, she told herself. She was tensed up, all nerves, and furious with Giles for being ill at such a time. The disappointment of not being able to watch the concert was too distressing to think about. But Giles had sounded so ill, so utterly wretched. She pitied him. Sighing deeply as she drove along the country road, Francesca remembered how she had once heard her mother telling someone, 'Giles Sutherland will be a fine man once he gets away from the influence of his parents.'

But Giles had never really got away; instead, he had gone into business with them. An economic merger, he had called his marriage. There was nothing so cold as economics, thought Francesca with just a hint of relish.

Within twenty minutes she reached the house. She drove straight up to the entrance and parked the car. Then she got out and found it was raining. The house looked even more grim and foreboding. Frowningly, she made her way to the door. There was a light in the vast hall, also on the staircase. She went to the foot of the stairs and called rather shakily, 'Giles! Giles, are you upstairs?'

'Yes. Come up, Francesca.'

He still sounded breathless. She hurried up the stairs two at a time and then paused to glance along the wide balcony. A beam of light stole out from the half open door at the end and she hurried towards it.

'Giles?' She gently pushed the door open wider, peered in.

'Thank God you've come, Francesca!'

She stepped into the room, conscious of its elegance, the deep-piled carpet beneath her feet, the soft blue drapes and the concealed lights which threw a pale glow on to the bed where Giles lay propped up against his pillows. She thought he looked wild and unruly and far too hot. His eyes were feverishly bright, his breath came too quickly.

'You certainly don't look very well,' she said as she crossed to the bedside. 'I must telephone your doctor, Giles.'

He held out his hand, but she ignored it. 'Will you get me a drink?' he said, withdrawing his hand again. 'I'm so dry.'

'Yes, I will. Who is your doctor, Giles? I must telephone him at once. You look as though you have a fever.'

Giles shook his head. 'A drink,' he said again. 'I've seen the doctor. He came over this morning and told me I had a virus. I've got some tablets.'

Francesca straightened up. Too angry to speak, she drew away. 'Then why did you ask me to come over?'

she said at last and in a tight, constrained voice. 'Are you worse? Should I ring him again?'

'No, no. I just want you to get me a drink. Then come and talk to me.' His eyes were imploring. 'I couldn't stop thinking about you, Francesca.'

'What did the doctor say?' Francesca's eyes were hard and unflinching.

'I've told you, it's a virus. He says I'll be better in a couple of days if I stay in bed and take the antibiotics.'

'Didn't he want to speak to your wife?'

'Of course not. He knew she was away.'

Levelly Francesca told him, 'I was listening to Adam.'

Giles fingered the sheet. 'I thought you might be.'

'Might be!' She stared at him aghast. 'But this is his big night. Aren't you interested?'

Giles raised his eyes to her. 'Should I be?' he asked, and this time there was a numbness about his voice that made Francesca lower her eyes. He obviously knew what was going on between his wife and his friend.

'I'll get you that drink,' she said quickly. 'I expect there'll be some squash in the kitchen.'

'Please.' Giles ran his tongue over his dry lips, and turned his head on to his shoulder in a weary gesture. 'I would like a drink. I'd get up, but I feel so weak.'

He had always been weak, Francesca thought as she hurried downstairs again. Why didn't he bother to assert himself? He was pathetic. As for her night, it was ruined. She felt miserable and ill at ease looking about Celia's kitchen, like some kind of thief in the night. She hated the house, she despised its occupants. All the same, she searched until she found a bottle of lemon squash and after making an iced drink she took it up-stairs to Giles.

'You look very tight-lipped,' he said, avoiding her

eyes and taking the drink. 'I know you're furious with me. But everyone is away. We're all alone.' He gave Francesca a sly smile. 'So why shouldn't we be together? I'm not in a position to do you any harm.'

'Would you like me to telephone your wife?' Francesca asked deliberately, glancing now at the mirrored wall at the head of the bed and at the fabulously expensive furniture units. 'I could do that.'

'You know Celia won't be back tonight, Francesca. You know where she is, who she's with.' He laughed a little wearily. 'There's no need to look so nervous. You're not exactly walking on holy ground. Celia lives somewhere along at the other end of the balcony. She never comes into this room.'

'You're ill, and she is your wife. I must phone her.'

'No!' His tone sharpened. 'I'll be all right, Francesca. Mrs Coates will be back first thing in the morning.'

'You mustn't get out of bed, Giles. Do as the doctor told you. Have you got your tablets?'

He nodded. 'My own personal pills. They're under my pillow.'

'Could you eat anything?'

He shook his head.

'I'll make a large jug of lemon for you,' Francesca told him, 'then I must get back. I can't stay here, Giles. I feel embarrassed.'

'But we've known each other for so long, since we were children.' He raised his hand again. 'I want to hold you, Francesca, even if it's only for a moment. Please.'

'Really, you are a most selfish man,' Francesca said quickly, and as her heart filled with compassion for the man she had once imagined she had loved, 'I don't want your virus, Giles. I've told you, I'm a working woman. I haven't time to lie in bed.'

He closed his eyes and did not open them again until Francesca had reached the door. 'Francesca!' he called after her, and raised himself up a little. 'Somehow I'm going to make you love me again ... Somehow ... You'll see.'

She smiled back at him. 'Keep warm,' she whispered across the room. 'And don't look so desperate, Giles. You've just got a chill. You're not going to die.'

'I feel like dying every time I think of what I've lost,' he told her, sinking back on to his pillows again. 'I was the world's biggest fool, Francesca.' He smiled faintly again. 'But then pity is akin to love. I can count on your sympathy at least, can't I, Francesca?'

This time Francesca could not speak; the happier times she had spent with Giles came crowding back into her mind. And her mother had liked him. 'I must go,' she said, and turned to the door. 'If I drive fast I might just get back for the grand finale.'

'Don't wait up for Adam,' Giles murmured. 'He'll not come back tonight, Francesca. Believe me, Francesca, men of genius and women like Celia are truly liberated. Don't sit among the cinders. Believe me, Adam Greco is no Prince Charming. Besides, men like him are very wary of girls like you, Francesca. They want no ties. They don't need love. And Celia—she's no fool. She doesn't expect Adam to love her.'

Numbly Francesca turned to stare back at him. 'Do you hate Adam?' she asked in a small voice.

Giles shook his head. 'No,' he said calmly, 'I could never hate a man like Adam. I admire him. He's strong and clever and he just takes what he pleases. Besides, Celia has a good business head and she'll not leave me.'

Adam Greco is a celebrity, but he's not a millionaire.'

'And you are?'

He closed his eyes. 'Very soon I may well be. Our money works for us,' he told her wearily. 'It must get very tired.'

Like a ghost, Francesca crept from the house. She did not remember the drive back, but once in the sitting room at Old Beams she wandered desolately about the room thinking of what Giles had told her. He was right, of course. Adam would be surrounded by exultant admirers, musicians intoxicated by his success, women attracted by his dark good looks. There would be reporters, agents and Celia would be there. Giles for once had brought her to her senses.

With a sigh of acceptance, Francesca stood staring absently at the hostess trolley. It would not be needed. She was not hungry; she would make herself a drink, sit by the fire for a while. She moved to the window and looked pensively out. The rain had stopped and the moon, like a slim golden canoe, rose on rapid-fast clouds. The wind had got up and above the wind came the screech of a wild animal prowling out somewhere on the black crags above the windswept crest of the forest. A badger, Francesca decided calmly, for she was familiar with the eerie night sounds. She was not afraid to be alone in the old house. Old Beams was for her a kind of sanctuary; she felt her mother's guiding spirit within its walls, a love which guided her. A love which she knew now could never die, nor rest.

She was restless. She went to the kitchen and returned with her coffee, but she did not drink it at once. She thought of Adam again. The concert hall had been packed. His music was enjoyed by all age groups. Adam Greco's concerts were not stuffed-shirt affairs. His breadth of range took in everything from Mozart to Leonard Bernstein. Adam loved modern jazz; he loved beat; he loved all music.

If only he loved her! Francesca closed her eyes for a few moments. How dark and debonair he had looked. How leanly and yet strongly masculine he was. If only he loved her!

She would have to stop dreaming. Sipping her coffee now, she sat staring into the fire. The clock in the hall had already struck eleven. She must go to bed.

But she did not stir; instead she sat back and closed her eyes again; sad, wistful eyes, eyes which were beginning to grow moist. She slept for a while and then awoke with a start. She jumped up. The beams of a car's headlights fanned out across the wall of the room, and Francesca felt something like an explosion of joy in her brain. Adam was back! He had come home!

In a frenzy of joy she ran out into the hall. Then a sobering thought occurred to her. Would Celia be with him? And if she was, would they expect her to be safely tucked away in bed? Panicking now, Francesca turned to the stairs. She would undress, put on her dressing-gown, look as though she had got up at the sound of the car. She reached her bedroom just as the clock in the hall struck one.

'Francesca?'

It was Adam. He was alone and he had expected her to wait up for him. Giles had been wrong! She had been wrong! With a fresh rush of elation, and still struggling into her gown, Francesca went out on to the landing.

'Hello, Miss Lamb.' He was standing at the foot of the staircase, staring up at her, his dark eyes glinting mischievously. 'Well, didn't you miss me?'

In a few bounds Francesca was down the stairs, her arms about his neck, her eyes shining up into his. 'I missed you,' she choked. 'I've been waiting up for you.' Buoyant with happiness, she whispered, 'Are you hungry? I have a meal ready for you.'

'You are excited!' His smile was gentle as he put her away from him. 'Did you watch the concert?' As he spoke he drew off his fur jacket. 'I'm not hungry,' he said, 'but I would like a drink.'

Feeling calmer and a little ashamed of her unprofessional behaviour, Francesca hurried on ahead of him. 'I thought Celia might be with you,' she said stiffly. 'I expect you drove her straight to Thorneyburn House.'

'Yes.' Adam moved away to the shadows where a cabinet stood with the drinks. He poured one for himself and then turned to consider her with focused concentration. 'I'm glad you waited up for me,' he said thoughtfully. 'I'd been hoping you would.'

Francesca stared back at him. She thought he looked pensive, too calm, too cool for a celebrity who had just left the stage. 'Is there something wrong?' she asked, conscious of his scrutiny, conscious too of the racing of her heart. Perhaps he was wondering why she had flung herself into his arms. Perhaps she had embarrassed him. 'I'm afraid I did get carried away by the excitement of the evening,' she told him shortly. 'I'm not usually so emotional.'

'Of course not.' His underlip curved faintly, but he did not look at her.

'Aren't you hungry?' Francesca's voice shook a little as a new shyness crept over her. 'I have some food ready for you.'

He raised his eyes now; eyes bright with amusement.

Stepping up to the fireside, he teased, 'I drive all this way back as quickly as I dared, and you talk of food!'

'I'm sorry.'

'And I'm sorry ... I apologise for my selfishness, Francesca. You do this for me and I'm not grateful.' He laughed softly and moved towards her. 'You know,' he said gently, 'I missed you. In fact, I cursed myself for not taking you along with me.'

'Taking me? She looked at him, stupefaction in her gaze. 'But you took Celia.'

'For a very different purpose. I had something else in mind when I thought of you, Francesca.'

'Oh, I see.' She turned away on a deep, unhappy breath. 'If you don't really want anything, then I'll go to bed.'

'Nonsense! I want to talk to you. Perhaps I am hungry. Yes, we'll dine together, Francesca. You can tell me what you thought of my concert.'

'You were a great success,' Francesca said swiftly as she turned to the trolley. How could she tell him that she had missed his performance, that she had been at Thorneyburn House with Giles? 'We're all very proud of you.'

'You saw me in colour?' Adam's dark eyes glittered again. 'How did I look? You must tell me, Francesca. Did you approve of my silk shirt? Celia bought it for me.' He caught her expression and his jocularity faded. He frowned as he drew a chair up. 'Actually,' he went on, 'I wasn't happy with things tonight, Francesca. I didn't quite bring it off. Of course the young set liked the Bach. But it was my concerto I was interested in, and it wasn't quite right. There was something missing.' He sighed deeply as he turned to gaze into the fire again. 'Something wrong.'

'I'm sure it was wonderful,' Francesca told him swiftly, wanting him to forget the concert now. 'I don't suppose you're ever wholly satisfied with a performance. You're much too critical of yourself.'

He gave her a long look, smiled and then sat down. 'You're having something with me, aren't you?' he said.

Francesca smiled, knowing full well that an inner excitement would stop her from eating. 'I'll certainly have some coffee.'

She served out his meal and then sat back to watch him enjoy it. A congenial silence filled the room and the fire purred approvingly. Later Francesca watched Adam select a cigar and then sit back to puff the rich smoke up into a cloud about his face. He looked happy and relaxed, and again they sat in silence for a while.

'You must be very tired,' Francesca whispered at last.

He raised his eyes. 'And what about you, Francesca? Aren't you tired?'

'I'm all right. Is there anything else I can do for you?' She moved the trolley away to one side as she spoke, then the small low table.

Without answering her he got up and put a tape on the turntable of his record player and almost at once the room was full of a gentle, sweet kind of music. It had a mediaeval flavour, the recorder being predominant. 'Leave that,' he said as Francesca began to clear away. 'Come and sit down beside me, Francesca.' He took her hand and drew her to his chair. 'Sit down on the rug. Listen to this hauntingly sweet sonata.'

Francesca sat with her back against his chair, her gaze on the fire, her eyes full of surprise, her heart beating fast now with an exciting alarm. Something in his attitude had made her decide that it would be churlish to refuse.

They sat in the firelight for a while listening to the soft music, enjoying the warmth and shared peace, and then Francesca felt her whole being stir with some agonizingly joyous sensation. She caught her breath; she did not dare move as Adam now ran his fingers through her hair. They reached the warm skin at her nape and then in a clever, disciplined way began to play across her soft skin. The sensation was so beautiful, so electrifyingly exciting; she felt a shudder of pure ecstasy thrill through her. Still she did not move. She closed her eyes. She knew that he barely knew he touched her. Again Adam was lost in his world of music. He was using her as some kind of instrument of relaxation. In some way contact with her eased his tensed-up nerves. She comforted him, but she by no means stirred up his passion. And strangely enough she did not resent this, it made her in some small way part of him, part of his success. She tried hard to listen to the music, to ignore the contact of his skin. But his forefinger and thumb moved to the lobe of her ear, and this contact was too too much for her. The blood rushed to her head. She turned to stare up at him, her eyes full of alarm.

Adam stared back at the girl who sat at his feet, 'Francesca,' he whispered as he drew her up on to his knee. 'Tell me, did you wait up for the celebrity? Or did you wait up for me?'

The hard warmth of his arms about her was too much for Francesca. In a frenzy of emotion she pressed herself against him. More than anything now she wanted to rouse in Adam some of the passion she felt herself. Her eyes shone, her lips parted. It was like being caught in an invisible and tightening noose; she could not free herself. Nor did she want to be free. 'Adam,' she whispered, and as though confounded by her own be-haviour she shook her head a little. 'Adam, kiss me. Kiss me the way you kiss Celia.'

She had said the wrong thing. Instantly she had felt him tense. In alarm she watched his dark eyes narrow. 'Adam,' she whispered again, terrified now by what she saw in his eyes and in the hard way he had set her away from him, roughly pushed her to her feet. 'Adam, I——'

She felt his hands hard on her shoulders, she could not go on, nor could she look at him, so she did not see his eyes soften and then close wearily. 'Francesca,' he said, and his breath came harshly, 'would you have me destroy you? Turn my very fine housekeeper into an accommodating one?'

Just for a moment Francesca looked up into his steady, faintly amused eyes, then with a little cry she turned and fled from the room. Dazed with remorse, she paced her bedroom for a while, then flinging herself on to her bed, she at last fell into a merciful sleep.

CHAPTER SIX

MORNING came and with it a new terror for Francesca. How was she to go down and start her work as though nothing had happened? How foolish she had been, how stupid! If only Adam had played something less melancholy, less moving. If only she had not got so worked up, carried away. Now she felt dizzy with remorse, almost afraid to go down.

The autumn sun streamed into her bedroom with its cool audacity and she smiled and took heart and told herself that Adam would have forgotten her passionate outburst. He was well used to adoration. She would go down and pretend that she had slept soundly, act as though there was nothing on her mind but the running of the house. The morning papers would have arrived and that would help. Adam would be engrossed with what the critics had to say about his composition.

Wearing her corded jeans and a brown, roll-necked sweater, Francesca went downstairs. To her surprise she found Adam already in the kitchen. He had finished his breakfast and was now reading the papers, drinking his coffee.

'Well,' he said, glancing up as Francesca came into the room, 'the critics don't exactly hate me,' he laughed. Then he smiled and drawing up a chair said, 'Good morning, Francesca. Come and sit down. The coffee is still hot. We've all had breakfast.'

Francesca could not speak for a moment, then she said quickly, 'I see I've slept late. I'm sorry, I didn't realise.' She poured herself some coffee and sat down opposite to him.

'Sugar?' Adam smiled across the table at her. 'Celia rang,' he told her. 'Giles isn't too well. The doctor's looking in this morning. I said I'd go across.'

'Poor Giles,' Francesca whispered as she looked down into the coffee as she stirred it. 'He never seems very fit.'

'He's all right,' Adam said sharply, sitting back to stare at her. 'Celia's been away, so I expect he's sorry for himself again. I've never met such a melancholy man. At times I have no sympathy for my friend.'

He stood rather abruptly and Francesca raised her eyes to admire his black shirt and tan and white houndstooth jacket.

'Is there anything I can do?' she asked nervously.

'There's nothing anyone can do,' Adam returned in a tired tone. 'Giles seems determined to punish some-one. Sometimes it's himself, at other times Celia. It's a good thing she's made of sterner stuff. I'm afraid he infuriates me. I lose patience.' He strode away, then turned to say gently, 'It was charming of you to wait up for me last night, Francesca. Somehow I knew you would.'

Francesca lowered her eyes, very conscious of his presence, of the way in which he was staring down at her. Then to her amazement she felt his lips lightly touch her cheek and she turned to him in alarm and feeling suddenly as though she wanted to cry.

'Another small tribute made respectable by the light of day,' he teased. 'To my faithful little housekeeper.' His lips curved provocatively and his eyes glittered mischievously as he inclined his head a little. 'My charming, sentimental Francesca. May she long keep her reason.'

Francesca lowered her eyes again. 'Do you want me to leave?' she asked soberly.

'Leave?' He frowned at her, his eyes puzzled. 'I want you to stay for ever, Francesca. Why the devil should I want you to leave?'

Perhaps he had forgotten? Of course he had. How could a man like Adam Greco take her seriously? He was merely teasing her, in a good mood. 'You were a great success,' she said breathlessly. 'I was very proud.' Suddenly she was very parched and she drew up her coffee again.

'A critical success,' he laughed as he began to stride about the room, the paper still in his hand. 'But there was something not quite right, Francesca. Something I didn't quite pull off.' He turned to frown at her, a frown which turned into a deep concentration. 'The next time, perhaps.' He relaxed again and came back to the table. 'I've made up my mind about something, Francesca,' he went on. 'You're coming along to my next concert. I want to see you there.'

'See me?' She raised wide eyes and her heart beat fast as a gust of emotion swept over her. 'Whatever for?' she whispered, willing herself to sit still, keep calm. 'Won't you take Celia again? She looks so good. And Giles, of course. Perhaps he'll be well enough next time.'

This time Adam threw back his magnificent head and laughed. 'No doubt they'll be there,' he chuckled. 'And, of course, Celia would encourage any man. But I have another reason for wanting you to be there, Francesca. You can help me.'

'Help you?' Francesca's words died away as another

idea shook her. 'How?' she demanded, and now her voice was strong with the strength of her anger. Her eyes were bright, her chin raised and childishly cantankerous.

Adam inclined his head as he stared down at her. 'You know,' he said as he raised his hand and ran a finger down her cheek, 'for someone so sweet you have a ridiculously suspicious mind.'

Francesca looked away from him. 'You mean you want a decoy,' she said icily. 'You don't want the press to get on to Celia. They wouldn't notice me—or at least they couldn't imagine anything about us.'

'Francesca!'

The harshness of his voice made her wince. She had said too much. A wave of terror ran down her back.

'I answer to no man,' he said evenly and with suppressed fury. 'Nor to any woman. I try to help Celia. Who wouldn't? But then I don't exactly treat you as a housekeeper, Francesca. You must realise that.'

'I realise that I'm your housekeeper,' Francesca said in a small voice. 'And that you wouldn't die without me.'

Their eyes met and clung and then he was smoothing her hair again and drawing her head gently to his breast. 'Don't let's get upset,' he said calmly. 'But let me tell you this, Francesca. I was compelled to send you off to your bed last night. Your sweet, natural kisses have more power in them than you can imagine. But you mustn't ask me to cheat. All I have to offer a girl like you is my music, my talent.' He drew away gently and with a lowered, 'But then I couldn't expect you to understand that.' He frowned suddenly and his tone changed. With energy he said, 'I must go. Celia will wonder what's keeping me.'

'Adam?' She reached out to him. But already he had reached the door and for some reason he did not look back. And to Francesca it seemed that he had told her that he could love her, but that he would not, all in one breath. For a while she stared at the door, as though gazing after someone who had just gone on a long journey, wondering if he would ever come back. Then, slowly, she got up and faced the reality of a day's work.

All morning she answered the telephone to the press, dealing confidently with their inquiries, tactfully putting them off when necessary. There were congratulatory notes to be written down from envious but friendly colleagues, many ordinary people, too, just telephoning to say how much they had enjoyed the concert. After lunch, Francesca was glad to get out of the house, leaving Mrs Noble to clear up, and Mr Noble still clearing leaves but now warmly clad in a woollen hat which left only his ears protruding like some kind of rosy fungi. It was November now and the days were short, and Francesca knew that the snow could come at any time and that her trips to the cottage would be curtailed. She would walk over the fields today, she decided, because she felt strangely elated, almost joyous, and almost as though her mother had still been there and she was going off to tell her all. Thorneyburn Cottage had become for Francesca like some lonely wayside shrine. Within its four large rooms she talked to herself, made plans, relived memories.

Today she stood staring at the bedroom wallpaper, remembering the very day when she and her mother had struggled together to get it evenly on to the not so straight walls. She wandered out into the little garden and stood for a while staring down at the dark, tattered patches of springy roots which in summer she knew would blossom into a living tapestry of Romilly, Vagans, Silver Queen. Her mother had loved the heathers. Francesca still remembered all their names.

Somehow she would get Thorneyburn Cottage back; somehow she would make it her home again. She would save and save. Giles would at least see that she got the chance of buying the place. A smile touched Francesca's lips. If Adam Greco preferred to admire her from afar then he would one day be in a position to do so. Simple, natural kisses, indeed! With the fading light her thoughts grew grey. A cloud of doubt now lowered over her. Because she was old-fashioned, Adam Greco had not wanted to hurt her. For him, romance was just something that lurked in a foolish girl's mind. With a few cleverly chosen words he had restored her self-confidence, that was all. His music was not for her. His gift was for the world. As for women, for him there were all the Celias.

She would not allow herself to be seduced by self-pity, Francesca told herself, and she marched back into the cottage kitchen, making her plans as she went. Even if she was forced to leave Old Beams one day she would still travel back from wherever she was working to spend regular periods at Thorneyburn Cottage. It would, one day, belong to her. No one would intrude on the memories, the love stored in that little house. With a loving gesture, she ran her fingers over the sneck of the door and then quickly turned to go. It would soon be twilight and already there was a faint sprinkling of snow on the high fells. She must lose no time in getting back.

Back at Old Beams Francesca quickly washed and then changed into her long tartan skirt and a yellow blouse. She stirred up the fire in the dining room and waited anxiously for Adam to leave the sitting room and come in for dinner. She fixed him a drink. But still he did not come. She went to the hall and looked about. The light was still beneath his door; he was still working. Just as she was about to turn away again, the sitting room door opened and he came out.

'I've poured you a drink,' Francesca told him, and gave him a quick smile. 'Dinner is ready too.'

'You've got a good colour.' He gave her a smile. 'Been tramping the fells again?' He seemed amused.

Francesca nodded as he passed her and went straight to the fire.

'How is Giles?' she inquired, fighting hard to hide her sudden shyness. 'I hope he's feeling better.'

'Naturally,' he answered sharply. 'He's feeling very much worse.' He picked up his drink. 'But that was to be expected. The damn fool's been at Mrs Coates' tablets again. He's determined to cause a scandal.' He finished his drink with one gulp and then looked looked directly into Francesca's startled eyes. 'If he doesn't manage that, then I'd say he'll turn violent.'

'But I thought he was ill? I thought he had 'flu or something like that.' Francesca's voice trembled.

Ignoring her, Adam ran on, 'He doesn't seem to realise he's not the only man in the world to suffer disappointment, disillusion. God knows, he's fortunate enough. He has money—and Celia. They're not ridiculously in love, but they have some kind of understanding.'

'A financial one.' Francesca's tone was a little sneering 'Could anything be colder?' she retorted as she went to busy herself at the table.

'What makes you say that?' Adam's eyes followed her questioningly.

She shrugged her shoulders. 'I don't know,' she returned, feeling suddenly insolently alive. 'As you say, they're not madly in love with each other. Anyone can see that.' She pulled her mouth, shrugged her shoulders again. 'Why don't they have children?' she threw flippantly. 'Then they could at least love their children. Or would Celia Sutherland not want to risk losing her figure?'

He looked at her as though his own heart had turned to stone. 'I will not have you talking that way,' he said in a cold measured voice. 'You're making a grave mistake, Francesca. In fairness to Celia I must tell you that it's Giles who's not in a position to father children. I just wish he could take this misfortune like a man and stop brooding. Why must he be so depressed?' In an agitated fashion Adam paced the floor. 'Sometimes I wonder,' he went on darkly, 'if my friend's actions are quite normal. Why does he want sleeping pills? He sleeps well enough. Why must he be continually drawing attention to himself in this morbid manner?' He drew himself up and paused to stare at the fire. 'Yes,' he said grimly, 'I find myself worrying more and more about Giles.'

Poor Giles! Francesca drew away, anxious now to conceal her own feelings. At one time Giles had been a happy young man. And now? Was he so utterly embittered, so miserably disappointed? She turned back to glare at Adam. Even if Giles had no love for Celia that did not say that he was happy about Adam Greco going off so often with his wife. She felt angry suddenly. 'I expect Giles worries about you too,' she said hotly and with accusing eyes. 'Perhaps he doesn't really approve of you being seen so much with his wife?'

Adam frowned and then laughed. 'I see there's nothing I can say to convince you,' he said lightly. 'Your sympathy definitely lies with Giles, Francesca. I'm not surprised. From the moment you two met I saw that you and he had a kindred spirit, some kind of understanding.' He began to walk again, his hands firmly in his pockets. 'You may not believe me,' he went on, raising his eyebrows and giving her a swift glance, 'but I believe that I help their marriage. I think of myself as a bit of a crutch. Believe me, I don't intend to let Celia down. If anyone needs me, she certainly does.'

He paused to take up his drink and then went to his seat by the fire, and watching him closely Francesca thought how grave and stern he looked. It was jealousy that lashed her into action, jealousy that wrung the truth from her. 'I'm afraid I don't feel any admiration for Mrs Sutherland,' she said angrily. 'I think she has you completely under her spell. In fact, I wouldn't be surprised if she's already made up her mind to have a talented child. Women like Celia Sutherland plunder where they choose.'

Adam turned to stare at Francesca and a frightening pallor spread out beneath his skin. His eyes were very dark now, almost black, and deathly still. Francesca moved back a little, her heart racing, wishing once again that she had been able to control her feelings. There was something in his concentration that scared her; something in the contemptuous twist of his mouth that made her want to turn and run. Even his voice had changed; it was like the voice of some other man as he told her scathingly, 'Do I look the kind of man to be seduced by a woman? Even with all your naïveté, Miss Lamb, you must know that a man like myself chooses the woman whom he wishes to mother his children. Celia must fulfil her destiny. I must fulfil my own.'

Their eyes met and for all his arrogance Francesca knew that she still loved Adam Greco. No moral reins held this man; he took and did as he pleased. Yet she loved him. 'I'll serve dinner,' she whispered. 'Will you sit down?'

He crossed to the table and stood glancing over it. 'We'll sit down together,' he said, giving her a reassuring smile. 'And as fate has thrown us together,' he went on coaxingly, 'let's continue to enjoy ourselves. I must tell you about the rest of my concerts, Francesca. We're going to be very busy, but we'll have a break at Christmas. We'll dress the old house up. Perhaps we'll have a party.' He smiled at her as she moved about the table. 'Would you like that?' he asked.

Francesca put a bowl of French onion soup before him, and then sat down herself. But she could not speak. Like some deadly octopus Celia Sutherland already had one tentacle firmly secured upon Adam and very soon he would be in her entire power. As for Giles, she would be a fool to waste her sympathy on him. In the past Giles had had no thought for her feelings.

'Is there something wrong?' Adam leaned forward a little, raised his eyebrows. 'I must say this soup is delicious, Francesca. You're an excellent cook.'

Most raw country girls are, she wanted to hurl at him, but this time she managed to control the impulse.

'You're very quiet?' Adam frowned a little now.

She toyed with her spoon. I was thinking about the old days,' she told him quietly. 'The other Christmases.'

'Good gracious!' He sat back and laughed. 'When you're as old as I am, Francesca, you'll be able to talk about the old days. You're a mere child.' He leant forward again. 'A strange, enchanting child.'

She did not want his easy compliments. 'When is the next concert?' she asked.

'Three weeks' time, in London this time. And you're going with me, Francesca. I've made up my mind about that.'

Francesca raised her eyes. 'Do you imagine that I haven't one?' she asked levelly.

'You are touchy tonight!' He stared at her a little impatiently. 'Tell me, Francesca,' he said smartly, 'what is it that's troubling you? Aren't you happy here at Old Beams? Am I deluding myself?' He shrugged his shoulders and sat back to stare speculatively at Francesca. 'Please tell me.'

She shook her head and then got up quickly to serve the rest of the meal. Somehow she had to pull herself together; she was fast becoming involved with things that were nothing whatever to do with her. 'I must be tired,' she said, forcing a little laugh. 'I shouldn't go for such long walks.'

'Have you been down to your favourite cottage again?' He sounded easier and he smiled appreciatively again as she set a plate before him.

'I have,' she told him nervously. 'And I've made my mind up about something, Adam. I'm going to buy Thorneyburn Cottage. More than anything else I want to live there.' Sitting down again, she added, 'I'm determined to buy it.'

'That shouldn't be so hard,' Adam said, and he looked up to give Francesca an assessing stare. 'The place belongs to Giles. I must speak to him about it.'

'It will take some time, of course,' Francesca rushed

134

on. 'I have some money, but I'll have to save a lot more.'

'Good,' Adam said, and this time he laughed. 'I'm glad of that. At least you're not going to fly away for a while. Knowing Giles,' he went on more soberly, 'you'll have to pay the full price. Giles gives little away. It's a family trait. That's how they made their money.'

'I wouldn't expect any favours,' Francesca swept on excitedly. 'But I don't suppose many people would want a house in the middle of a field,' she went on hopefully. 'It shouldn't cost that much.'

Deliberately Adam put down his fork and spoon. 'My dear child,' he said, frowning across the table at her, 'you sound positively ready to retire! Life is just opening for you. You're not going to bury yourself down there for ever, I hope. I imagined you wanted Thorneyburn Cottage for a weekend place. Perhaps for your family or your friends.'

'I have no family,' Francesca told him shortly. 'I had one or two girl friends in London, but they wouldn't want to come here. No,' she said, looking directly at him again, 'I want to live in the cottage. I want to make it my home. You were right, Adam, I am very much a country girl. I love the simple life.'

'Francesca, will you please stop looking so aggressive! You sound defiant and ridiculous. You're not feeling ill, are you? You look warm. You're sure you haven't got a temperature?'

'You think I'm ill merely because I've told you that I would like to buy Thorneyburn Cottage?' Her voice rose with agitation. 'You think that I should want nothing whatever for myself?'

'Of course not! Damn it all, you're putting me off my food. But you do fit in here at Old Beams, Fran-

135

cesca, and I don't see any need for you to go off and live down there. It's a damp hole, in any case. A lot would have to be done to it to make it habitable.'

'I'd be happy there. It would be like going home.'

'You're talking nonsense—dreaming, Francesca. You have no idea how rough it can be in such a place. There's no damp course, no electricity. Can you see yourself lighting paraffin lamps or dealing with Calor gas?'

'Yes, I can see myself——' Francesca's voice faded away as her thoughts wandered happily on.

'Let's take our coffee to the fireside,' he said, getting up for the coffee pot and pouring out the coffee before she could do so. 'You disappoint me,' he told her gruffly. 'I thought you had a feeling for this old place. I actually thought you liked us, the old place and me. Now you talk about buying a cottage and leaving us.'

'A girl must have her dreams,' Francesca told him as she moved to the fireside chair. 'I'm no exception.'

'Dreams of a husband, yes. A lover, perhaps.' He turned to frown even more deeply at her. 'I'm beginning to wonder if you have some dark secret, something to hide. Why in heaven's name should a girl like you want to live in a place like that? The world would go by, Francesca, and you would grow old.'

'We all grow old,' she returned calmly. 'None of us are the persons we were even yesterday.'

Her smile was so wistful, so sad, that Adam put his coffee down abruptly. He took her cup and saucer from her, set them down and drew her to him.

Francesca stared up at him in dismay; she had never seen him so intense, his brilliant eyes so strange and focused.

'Of course you'll grow old, Francesca,' he said in a

voice of constrained passion. 'The soft down of youth will go from your skin, the brightness will leave your eyes, your hair. But your spirit will never die, Francesca. I've captured it for ever. I've trapped it in a web of notes. Something of your beauty will never die. It will be here for ever. I'm going to make it so.'

'Me?' Francesca breathed, her lips trembling, her eyes wide, incredulous. 'How can I be in your music?'

'You'll see,' he said, and his eyes were very close to hers now. 'You'll see, Francesca. You'll never be able to leave me completely. I possess you, in a way you can never imagine.'

'I don't want to leave you, Adam.' Her eyes sought his, 'I want to tell you so much. I ...'

She was aware of being gathered up in his arms. Gently Adam kissed her, and then again. As they dropped down on to the sofa together nothing seemed to exist for each but the other.

'Adam?'

He kissed his name from her lips. 'Ssh,' he murmured, 'don't say a word.'

Francesca responded to his kisses, losing all notion of what she was doing. For the moment Adam held her close, as though he would never let her go, as though there was no other girl in the world. No Celia! For a precious moment she would cheat destiny, fool even herself. The moment belonged to her. Adam belonged to her; his dark skin, luxurious hair, his broad magnificent brow, his mouth. Francesca caught her breath as the tracing movement of his fingertips made her tingle with joy, grow tense and then cling to him in shy yet passionate desperation. She raised her eyes, her lips, parted them. Just for a second she saw some strange flash of joy in his eyes and then as he bore down on her there was only the sensation of drifting, an uncanny buoyancy and the most beautiful, almost unbearable ecstasy. She felt warm and ready, willing to be woven into a part of him ...

Then came the harsh, cruel sound of a car braking outside.

Francesca jerked up, reality gripping at her now. She looked at Adam and gasped with dismay.

It's all right,' he said gently, fastening the top button of her blouse with infinite tenderness, kissing her lightly and quickly again. 'Don't panic so, child.' Still smiling, he got up. 'There's no need for you to look like an escaped convict. It's only Celia. I know the sound of her car.'

Celia! The name was like a spear in Francesca's heart. She stood up. Engulfed in confusion, she fought to regain her calm. The spell was broken. Celia's distinct footsteps were in the hall. The door was flung open and she stood there, staring at them both in surprise.

'Dinner is late,' she said as she drifted into the room. She gave the trolley a contemptuous glance, then the table. For a moment her eyes lay coldly upon Francesca.

'How is Giles?' Adam asked stiffly, going for a cigar and then pouring a drink. 'No worse, I hope.'

'His cold is better,' Celia returned with a shrug of her slim shoulders. 'Otherwise he's just the same. Quite melancholy.' She sighed and then glanced at Francesca again. 'You'd better fix me a nice strong drink,' she said in a slow, deliberate tone. 'I certainly need something. Get your housekeeper one too, Adam, I think she's in for a shock. She looks as though she's going to cry, but then that's a trick of hers. In fact, Adam, our Miss Lamb is quite an actress. You're so right; she's not suited to her job. In fact I doubt whether she intends to remain a housekeeper long. The girl's ambitious.'

'What do you mean? Be careful, Celia.' Adam's broad brow gathered warningly. 'You sound as though you'd been drinking too much.'

'The only time I really drink is when I'm with you, darling. You know that. No, Adam, I'm dead sober. Dead sober when I tell you that your sweet, untouched by hand, spiritual little housekeeper is really quite a girl. You know, Adam, I hate to disillusion you, but your Miss Lamb couldn't even spare the time to watch your television appearance. She didn't hear a note of your music. Would you like to know why? She wasn't here. She was at Thorneyburn House with Giles. Now, what do you think of that?' Taking the drink which was still in Adam's hands, Celia went on coolly, 'Had Giles been well I just wonder what those two would have got up to.'

'I don't believe it. You don't know what you're saying.' Adam's voice was low and hollow, his eyes frighteningly solemn.

'Then ask Mrs Coates,' Celia laughed, and she turned to stare at Francesca, who now stood as white and as stiff as a statue, her heart beating like a startled leveret's. 'She happened to come back earlier than expected and she saw your Miss Lamb leaving the house. I didn't worm the confession out of Giles. I left him lying there like a melancholy calf, poor man.'

'I still don't believe it.' This time Adam's anger burned in his eyes. He took Celia by the arm, gripped it until she cried out. 'What are you up to, Celia? I know your talent for destruction.'

'You know all my talents, darling. So why look so upset? Still waters, you know, they still run deep.'

Pouting, she turned to Francesca again. 'I didn't come here to lecture,' she laughed mockingly. 'I'm not upset, so why should you be, Adam? I just don't intend to allow anyone to pull the wool over your eyes.' Smirking, she added, 'Apt, don't you think?'

Francesca stood silent. What could she say? If she spoke up and told Adam that she had once almost been married to Giles, everything would appear much worse. She had to keep that secret. She stepped forward, wincing at the doubt she saw in his eyes. If only she could have told him the truth, that she had known Giles Sutherland since childhood; that at one time she had almost married him. But no, that would not be wise, something warned her.

She said quickly, 'Mrs Sutherland is right, Adam. I did miss your concert.' She averted her eyes, unable to bear the shock she knew must now be registering in his. 'I was disappointed. I'm sorry.' She looked at him now with blue eyes wide and troubled. 'Giles did ring me,' she told him in a small voice. 'He said he felt very ill and begged me to go across. I couldn't refuse.'

'A worthy woman, no doubt.' Celia's green eyes glittered. She turned to Adam and laughed outright, then with a shrug of her shoulders told him, 'You really are in luck, Adam. As well as all her other endearing qualities it seems your Miss Lamb is also a nurse.'

Francesca could not speak. Numb with dismay, she stared at Adam. Am I a liar? she implored silently. But the doubt still lingered in his dark eyes and with a rush of despair she turned and ran from the room. Why, she panicked, did Celia Sutherland want to malign her? Did Celia truly love Adam? Had there been a hint of fear in those too bright eyes? And why, oh, why had Celia had to arrive at such a time! Francesca stumbled upstairs and once in her bedroom she banged the door shut and flopped down on the side of the bed. Reeling with emotion, she wondered what would happen now. As she thought over the scene an even more shocking idea occurred to her and, stunned, she sat perfectly still. Like Celia, she knew that she would have been prepared to give herself to Adam Greco, give herself without question, without any expectation of love or marriage. She loved the man so much! More than herself. She stood up again, braced herself. Whatever happened she would not allow him to think of her as a girl who would go from one man to another.

Francesca paced the floor in agitation, wondering what to do next. Finally she went to the window and gazing out she grew calm. At last she smiled faintly. For somewhere over the lonely moors a cock crowed. Like herself, he was bewildered, confused. He crowed because the moon was white and full and because he too had imagined the sun to be up.

By morning Francesca had made up her mind; she must leave Old Beams. She would pack her case, walk down the old Wanny train line to the main road and get a lift to the nearest town. She would take her memories and go. Go for ever. To stay would only mean being destroyed again. Somehow she had to keep her pride, her self-respect. She must leave Adam Greco to his music, his public, and the Celias who must come into his life. She must leave Giles to his self-pity.

Half an hour later, she was ready to leave. She picked up her case and handbag and opening the bedroom door peered out. It was early; no one would yet be about. She tiptoed along the landing and then came to a sudden halt at the head of the stairs. The sitting room door was slightly open and filtering through it came the sound of music. Adam was up and already lost in his music. Francesca's heart beat very fast; she closed her eyes, gripped the banister rail more tightly. His playing was unbearably sweet, the slow phrases of a study she now knew well, pensively sad; each note clear-cut, poignant with feeling.

For a few heartbreaking moments Francesca listened, then she turned her eyes to the landing window. It was beginning to snow. The world would soon look very beautiful, and Adam's playing was beautiful too. How could she ever forget him or his music?

But she must. Steeling herself, she made her way quickly and lightly downstairs. She was half way across the hall and then everything seemed to happen at once. The telephone rang shrilly, cutting across her regained confidence. Adam stopped playing and in a moment he was at the door, staring at her in frowning puzzlement. Another door opened and Mrs Noble appeared.

'I'll answer it,' Francesca said wildly, dropping her case and taking up the receiver. It was Celia. 'For you,' she whispered. 'It's Mrs Sutherland.'

Without a word Adam strode forward. With one hand he took the receiver and with the other he gripped Francesca's arm. 'Wait,' he said in a firm voice. 'You're not going anywhere. I want to talk to you.'

Mrs Noble disappeared, the kitchen door closed again. Francesca tried to free herself, but found it impossible. She glared at Adam now. She saw his expression change suddenly, his head bow, his eyes close. She heard him curse under his breath, and then he was saying, 'Take hold of yourself, Celia. Keep calm. I'll be over right away.'

Something dreadful had happened; Francesca felt a

142

strange fear pricking at her spine. Yes, she read it in the dazed, grave eyes Adam now turned to her. She read it in every line of his face, his mouth. She held her breath as he momentarily covered his face with his hand. 'What's wrong?' she whispered. Then, because he did not answer her, she picked up her case. She would not weaken; whatever had happened it was no business of hers. She was going.

'Francesca!' The strength of his voice stopped her. He gripped her arm again as his eyes sought hers. 'Don't go,' he said. 'Whatever happens, stay until the end of my concert season. You said you would.'

'What's happened?' she breathed. She felt terrified for some reason. She could not fathom the look in his eyes. 'Is there something wrong?'

'There is,' he said gravely and took her firmly by the shoulders. 'Giles has given us a real shock—he's tried to kill himself. Fortunately Mrs Coates found him in time.'

'Oh, no!' Francesca began to shake. She was full of terror now. Poor Giles! She understood grief, her own had been overflowing. She knew disappointment. But this was too terrible to contemplate. Giles, the happy young man she had once teased and kissed. She covered her face with her trembling hands. For a moment she almost hated the talented, handsome Adam Greco who could not tolerate the fact that she might be as unprincipled as himself. She thought only of Giles Sutherland, the young man who had so often cheerily called to her mother, 'Come on, Mrs Lamb, jump in. It's time someone swept you off those feet.' And now this pitiful degradation. 'What happened?' she whispered brokenly. 'Tell me. I must know.'

'Mrs Coates found him in the bathroom,' Adam told

her in a level voice. 'He'd taken some pills. I suspect him of wanting to give us a shock, that's all. He was always fond of practical jokes, but he was never a brave man. And it must take a brave man to destroy himself.'

'He's unhappy,' Francesca whispered. 'Tormented by bitterness. He needs treatment.'

'Then I must see that he gets it,' Adam said stiffly and as he set her away from him. 'You may well decide to visit him again while I'm away, Francesca, and I'm not prepared to take that risk.'

Francesca raised her eyes to his, but instantly his eyelids were lowered and she could no longer see his expression. 'Adam,' she whispered unsteadily, 'you don't understand.' Suddenly overcome with emotion, she reached out and clung to him. 'You must listen to me,' she whispered. 'I have so much to explain.'

'This is hardly the time for explanations,' he said grimly, and roughly pushed her away from him. 'But I think, for both our sakes, you should stay on. Take your case upstairs again. We'll soon settle down to some other kind of relationship. At least I'll be able to keep a fatherly eye on you in future. You could well have been in serious trouble, Francesca. You don't know Giles the way I do.'

Francesca let him go. For a while she stood very still, then wearily she picked up her case and started upstairs again. Was she staying because of Giles? she wondered. Or was it true that she could not bring herself to leave Adam? Both devils in their own way, she thought with a rush of passion.

CHAPTER SEVEN

ALL day the house had been silent and empty. The Nobles, still unaware of what had happened at Thorneyburn House, had gone off to visit some friends in the village. Miserably, Francesca had gone from room to room thinking of Giles, thinking of how they had once been so devoted to each other, so happy. Now Giles was mentally sick while she herself was reduced to a sorrow beyond her years. As for Celia mischievously putting it into Adam's head that she had been stealing away to see Giles, that was unforgivable. Before she left Old Beams she would make sure that Adam knew the truth. One day soon she must go, she told herself with a determined bitterness. Adam was ready to believe anything Celia told him. He had asked her to stay, but he had pointed out that their relationship must change. Francesca smiled, but mirthlessly, wondering what it would be like to be treated as a real housekeeper. It was nice, though, to realise that Adam acknowledged the fact that there had been some kind of relationship. But the miracle of going back to live at Thorneyburn Cottage would never happen. In a week or two, when everything had settled down again, she would pack her bag and her memories and go for ever.

With these thoughts in mind, Francesca went to the dresser and reverently drew out her mother's little recipe book. She stood silently fingering it, slowly turning the tattered pages, smiling sadly. As she stood there she heard the heavy steps of Adam in the hall and quickly put the book back in the drawer again. At once her heart was racing, her knees weak. She smoothed down her hair, took a deep breath and went out to the hall. Adam had gone into the dining room and she followed him into the room, her face pale, her eyes anxious. Without a word she watched him pour himself a drink and take it to the fireside. Then, sensing her presence, he turned to look at her.

'How is Giles?' Francesca whispered. 'What happened?'

He eyed Francesca curiously for a few moments. Then he said levelly, 'Giles? You always refer to Celia as Mrs Sutherland, Francesca.'

'Mr Sutherland, then. Does it matter?' Francesca's cheeks flamed with anger. His words had been like a caution and she felt infuriated.

'Nothing happened.' He turned back to the fire. 'Giles is going to be perfectly all right. He needs treatment, of course. At least that fact is now painfully obvious. I must admit that I didn't expect him to break down like this.'

'I'd like to tell you why I felt I had to go over to Thorneyburn House that night, Adam ... Mr Greco.' Francesca began to stammer a little beneath the harsh gaze he now turned upon her. 'There's so much I should tell you.'

He raised his glass and then finished his drink with one gulp. 'Did I ask you to explain?' he said swiftly, and his eyes swept critically over her. Then he smiled and told her more gently, 'Perhaps I was disappointed, Francesca. I'd tried so hard to capture something of you in my concerto. I'd imagined that you would recognise it. But then it's perhaps just as well that you didn't, for it wasn't exactly a success.'

'Adam!' Francesca ran to him, reached out to him.

His firm hands set her quickly aside. He smiled again, but strangely and studying her face in every detail as he did so. 'You little guessed, Francesca, but you truly inspired me. You were music, a joy. I wasted no time in getting back to you.'

'Oh, Adam! Will you listen to me?' Francesca flung her slim body against him this time, raised her arms to his neck, opened wide beseeching eyes.

But again and even more firmly he set her aside. There was no kindliness in his eyes as he told her, 'Celia is a practical, clear-sighted woman, Francesca. She doesn't suffer from illusions; she's not easily beguiled. She knows how to enjoy life in spite of everything. I must listen to Celia. She may even yet save me from complete disaster.'

Francesca would not let him finish. 'From what?' she burst out, her eyes wildly defiant now. 'From the truth?' On a torrent of fury and frustration she rushed on, 'Oh, Adam, why won't you listen to me? You don't really know me. You don't understand your friend Giles.'

'Oh, I understand Giles perfectly well.' His smile was cynical and cold. 'What would you have me do? Comfort him?'

'He needs comforting.'

'Perhaps.' Adam poured himself another drink. 'I should have guessed that he would like you to comfort him, Francesca.' He stared morosely at the drink as he swivelled it around in the glass. 'Remember,' he said, and his eyes were infinitely grave as he turned back to fix them on her, 'Giles doesn't happen to be your problem, Francesca.'

'I'd be sorry for any man in his position,' she told

him, roused again, holding his gaze unflinchingly. She read the doubt in his eyes and rushed on with, 'I'll pray to God that he'll soon be well again.'

'Celia is not in an enviable position either,' Adam said slowly. 'That's why I must ask her to come and stay here with us at Old Beams for a while, Francesca.' He raised his eyebrows as he went on, 'I hope you'll be generous enough in the circumstances to forget her wild accusations. She was worked up, and terribly shocked.'

'Yet you still believed her?' Francesca's voice was barely audible. 'You now have reservations about me, Adam.'

'I have reservations about Giles,' he cut in fiercely. 'But then I always had. As for trying to kill himself, or at least putting on a show of doing so, that was despicable. Whether he's having a breakdown or not I'm going to find that hard to forgive.'

'Where is he now?'

'He's gone off to hospital. Celia went with him. A Mr Sinclair is looking after him—a top man in that field.'

'And Mrs Sutherland is coming to Old Beams?' Francesca's voice was scathing, almost hostile.

'That's right, Francesca.' Adam's voice was crisp and businesslike again. 'We must do our best for her. I'm afraid Mrs Coates was in a terrible state. She's gone to stay with her sister down in the village for a while.'

'Very well, Mr Greco.'

The room was strangely silent for a few moments. Adam crossed the room and, reaching out, he took Francesca's cold hand in his own. 'Come now,' he said, and his voice was gentle again. 'Nothing has changed here at Old Beams, Francesca. You're still going to call

148

me Adam and be my very special kind of housekeeper. Believe me, I can't see myself managing without you.'

Francesca raised her eyes to his. She ran the house well, saw to his needs. Of course he could not do without her. But what about Celia? He could not do without her either. What did she do for him? She could not see Adam being patronising to a woman like Celia.

There was no time for retaliation, for at that moment the Nobles came into the room. They had heard the dreadful news. They were aghast, appalled. Poor Mr Sutherland! Such a nice, inoffensive man. Francesca raised her eyes to Mrs Noble's and read their unmistakable question: 'With such a wife how could any man survive?'

She shied away from the truth. Celia Sutherland merely had to crook her elegant finger and men like Adam Greco would rush to her aid. Yet Celia was capable of destroying both her husband's confidence and her lover's talent. But was Adam really Celia's lover? For a few numbed moments Francesca paused to stare at the man who had brought such confusion to her well laid plans. Then swiftly she turned and hurried from the room. Upstairs, she sat on the edge of her bed. She must stop thinking of herself, she decided. Somehow she had to go on encouraging Adam. His music was part of him; no one could stop her from worshipping his genius. She got up and walked slowly to the dressing table. Raising her eyes slowly, she smiled at her own reflection. Adam had said she was music and that he had captured part of her. Somehow she would capture part of him. With a wave of emotion Francesca suddenly covered her face with her hands. If only Celia had not been coming to Old Beams! With her in the house it was going to be difficult. Everything would change, Adam would change. But somehow, Francesca thought determinedly, clenching her small fists, she would see that he did not neglect his music. This would be her gift of love.

Everything did change. Within two days of Celia's arrival at Old Beams the old house seemed to take on a different character. Celia was like a brisk and unpleasant breeze ripping from room to room. The whole house seemed to shiver and shudder as every door was flung open and left, as Celia's resonant voice violated its most inner sanctuaries. The house seemed to breathe deeply and laboriously as her sharp feet smacked down the old staircase, it caught its breath as she outrageously flung open all the windows to allow the icy winter winds to gush in. Adam's time was fully taken up by driving her to hospital each day and by entertaining her in the evenings. There was no time for music. Francesca began to worry about Adam's next concert. With little to say she got on with her work. She prepared dinner each evening as usual, but even though Adam had protested vociferously she no longer sat down to eat with him. There were no nightcaps, no music and at ten o'clock Francesca found that she was glad to escape to her bedroom. At times she began to wonder if Adam had forgotten his concert. And always on Celia's face was that expression of greed and desire.

Two weeks before his concert Adam began to play again. Francesca was sorting some fruit on the kitchen table when she heard the first strains of music filtering through the house and with a gasp of joy she ran out into the hall. Tears rushed to her eyes. A rush of gladness filled her whole being. Then she heard Celia coming downstairs and something in her manner made Francesca look at her again. Celia looked even more

beautiful, even more confident. There was a look of
both scorn and triumph in her eyes as she strode flaunt-
ingly by Francesca. She looked like a woman who knew
that she was playing her cards with infinite skill, a
woman who knew she could not lose. Francesca lowered
her eyes, as the sitting room door opened and she heard
Adam run his hands over the keys and then stop playing. A rich man's wife, she thought, and suddenly her
heart felt like a sponge. A famous man's mistress? Celia
took everything.

'That was divine, darling,' Francesca heard Celia
call. 'You are so wonderful, Adam. I just wish I knew
more about music. If only I hadn't this constant head-
ache!'

Francesca hurried back to her kitchen. Frantically
she tried to absorb herself in her work. But it was useless. She was no longer happy at Old Beams. She was
no longer happy walking across to the cottage. Only
that week she had heard Celia complaining charmingly,
'Adam, my darling, you simply don't know how to treat
your servants. You're much too nice, much too familiar.' It seemed, too, that her mother's loving spirit had
left her. She had the terrible feeling of loneliness, of
being deserted.

That afternoon, Francesca was surprised to see Adam
drive off without Celia and then going into the dining
room she saw that Celia was dressed to go out. She was
wearing a black and white suit and a magnificent red
fox fur hat.

'Oh, yes,' Celia said, turning at the door and flicking
her cool eyes over Francesca. 'I'd like to speak to you,
Miss Lamb. Adam has gone to visit Giles on his own
this afternoon. I'm going shopping in town. I'm determined to get something quite stunning for Adam's con-

cert and I haven't much time left. There are also one or two things I would like you to do for us.'

Drained of all strength, all hope, all happiness, Francesca fought to hold her head high. So Adam had completely forgotten that he had invited her to go to his next concert. Celia was to accompany him once again. Giles would be left again, safely locked up this time.

'For your information,' Celia went on with a knowing smile, 'my husband is going on very well. We don't need to worry about him. He's responding to a new drug and according to Mr Sinclair he won't need to stay with them very long.'

'I'm glad to hear it, Mrs Sutherland.' Francesca felt as though she had hauled the words from her throat. Anger and pride came to her rescue and she said much more forcibly, 'You'll no doubt be glad to get back to Thorneyburn House.'

Pursing her lips and regarding Francesca for a few moments, Celia said, 'And no doubt you'll be pleased to see me go.' She stood up very straight and a warning light flashed in her eyes. 'But let me tell you this, Miss Lamb. My husband may be a walkover for a girl like you.' Her lips lengthened contemptuously. 'Giles just wants a little kindness. But where Adam Greco is concerned you're merely making a fool of yourself. He's a man and you're out of his province. He's sophisticated and you're, forgive me, a peasant. It's better to face the truth.'

For a moment Francesca felt that she was crumbling inside. Then she had the mad impulse to hurl herself at Celia Sutherland and drag out her hair. For a moment she knew what hate was. She wanted to kill Celia. For a while the two women stared at each other in silence. Then Francesca took a deep breath and said in an amazingly cool voice, 'I'll go the minute I see that Mr Greco no longer needs me. I don't intend to be discarded by you, Mrs Sutherland.'

'What do you intend, Miss Lamb?' Celia laughed contemptuously. 'I wonder. Somehow I cannot credit you with being the cause of my husband's breakdown. Even poor Giles has taste.'

Francesca turned white before the woman who sought to degrade her. She clenched her hands, dug her nails into her palms. Anger throbbed in her head and yet she kept silent. Some even stronger emotion willed her to be cautious; it was almost as though she felt the strength of her mother's warm hand pulling her away from danger, urging her not to fall into any trap. She took a deep breath and said softly, 'You sound over-wrought, Mrs Sutherland. I'm sure you don't mean what you say. Please, if there's anything you would like me to do for you, just say.'

Celia's head jerked back in surprise, then her eyes narrowed suspiciously. 'You make me laugh,' she said with a sneer. 'Why shouldn't you have a rustic romp if you feel so inclined? As for Adam thinking you're an angel, that's ridiculous.' Her eyes flashed maliciously again. 'Unless he means that you're as tame as any angel must be.'

Francesca watched Celia stride from the room, then she hurried away to get on with her work. Something was going to blow up during the next few days, she felt sure of that. With a woman like Celia Sutherland in the house nothing could remain the same. Celia annoyed everyone with whom she came in contact in some sort of way. Frowningly Francesca folded and put away the laundry, then she went over to the cottage to see the Nobles for a short while.

It was after six when she came back to the house and she quickly set about preparing dinner. At half past six she heard Adam's car and at once her heart was racing again; she could not help herself.

'Oh, there you are, Francesca.' Adam smiled at her from the kitchen doorway. 'Will you come into the sitting room? I want to talk to you about my concert next week.'

Francesca stared back at him, her heart beating even more excitedly. Emotion flushed her face. She felt sure that he had remembered inviting her to his concert; he was going to remind her and make arrangements. Suddenly she was reeling with happiness.

As she reached the doorway Adam put his arm lightly about her waist and together they crossed the hall to the sitting room.

'I don't know how we'll ever make it up to you,' he said gently and as he turned to look gravely upon Francesca. 'You're a perfect housekeeper, Francesca. And I've been so happy with you in the house. You've been good to Celia too, and for that I'm also grateful. I know you don't exactly approve.' His dark eyes were gently questioning for a moment, his eyebrows rose and then his lips stirred into a smile.

Francesca felt that at any moment they would fall into each other's arms. 'Adam,' she whispered, her own eyebrows raised now, 'I wish you would let me talk to you. I have so much to tell you. There's so much you don't know about me and I no longer want to deceive you.'

He laughed softly. 'I know all I need to know, Francesca,' he murmured, and his eyes never left hers. 'I know how kind and generous you are, how unselfish.'

'You make me sound like an angel,' Francesca whispered back, a little apprehensive now. 'And just as boring!'

'What a dreadful thing to say!' He frowned at her in amazement. 'My dear Francesca, why must you pull yourself down as fast as I build you up? Have I offended you?' Are you still disgusted with my show of vanity? Can you not yet forgive me for preferring to think that you were here at Old Beams listening to me rather than sitting with poor sick Giles?'

'No.' She shook her head and because his eyes were so dark and burningly beautiful she suddenly fell against him and laid her cheek against his chest. 'I just miss you so,' she faltered. 'I see so little of you now, Adam. And what's even worse, I never hear you playing. What about your new composition, Adam? You were working so hard at it. You said,' she stood back again, raised her eyes shyly, 'I had inspired you. Were you telling the truth?'

'My dear child!' He set her back from him, his hands firmly upon her shoulders. 'Why in heaven's name should I lie? Of course you inspire me. You still do. Don't you concern yourself about my work. Believe me, Francesca,' he touched his head lightly, 'it's all in here. It will never leave me.' He smiled briefly and then changing his tone turned away from her and said more brusquely, 'It's the concert I wanted to talk to you about, Francesca. I have a week of rehearsals and so I must leave tomorrow.' He turned back to give her a long searching look. 'I must ask you to do something else for me.' He took her hands into his. 'I must ask you to look after Celia for me while I'm away. Believe me, I'll not worry so much if I know that she has a sane little person like yourself at her side. I'm afraid, Francesca, Celia may have a tough assignment ahead of her—I can't tell you more at the moment.'

Francesca drew her hands from his. As she stared at him she felt herself grow cold. So Celia Sutherland had completely enslaved him! When he had drawn her into the room he had been thinking only of Celia. Even now, his distant look was evidence that he was still thinking of her. For a few moments she could only stand staring numbly at him.

'I know you don't care too much for Celia,' he began again, his eyes sober. 'But do this for me, Francesca. Please.'

'I happen to be in your employ,' she answered. 'Had you forgotten? I'll do anything.' Above the pain of disappointment, the frustration which tore at her being, she heard him say lightly, 'Good. That's settled, then.'

'Anything else?'

Francesca's tone made Adam frown a little as he turned to look at her again. 'Yes,' he said, moistening his lips and looking puzzled at her show of valiance, 'there is one other thing, Francesca. I'm afraid Celia imagines she's coming to London with me. That's out of the question at the moment and I'm sure she's going to be very upset. That's why I've made up my mind to go in the early hours and so I must leave you to break the news. You can tell her that I'll telephone her each night.'

Francesca nodded and smiled as suddenly some of her spirits returned. 'I'll tell Mrs Sutherland. I'll break the news—I'm just the person to break bad news.'

He laughed this time and took her hand again. 'I'll ring my housekeeper too,' he said playfully. 'Just to make sure she's not out sick-visiting again.'

'Your next concert is to be televised, then?'

'Yes, it is.'

Francesca could see by his expression that he was not thinking of his concert now.

'You won't leave Celia alone too much?' he said, grave-eyed again.

'I don't intend to act as a chaperone,' Francesca returned sharply. 'After all, Mrs Sutherland is quite a big girl. Besides, just what do you imagine is going to happen to her?' Jealousy whipped the colour to her face again. 'Is she so very precious?'

Fierce little lights shot into his dark eyes as he turned to glare at her. 'Look after her,' he said gruffly. 'Whether you approve or not, just look after her until I get back. Then I hope it will no longer be necessary.'

What did he mean by that? Was he going to run off with Celia? Perhaps Celia and Giles were going to be divorced after all. Perhaps Adam was now rich enough to compete? Francesca looked up into Adam's steady eyes and suddenly she thought how tense he looked, how much older. How harsh! She nodded as memory robbed her of speech. The memory of the night she had waited up for him; the memory of his fingertips against her skin, fingertips capable of stirring the most thrilling music in her own heart and mind. She turned to go.

'Francesca?'

She could not turn and look at him, but as she closed the door she heard him run his hands over the keys of his piano and something in the sound brought a fresh rush of fear and frustration into Francesca's mind. Celia had broken Giles Sutherland. And now she was going to ruin Adam Greco! She had seen the anguish in his eyes. Already the wretched woman had dulled their brilliance. Already the laughter and happiness had gone from Old Beams—the music.

The telephone rang shrilly and Adam emerged from the sitting room. 'I'll take it,' he called gruffly. 'I'm expecting a call.'

Then Celia appeared and Francesca pausing on the second stair watched Celia brush her cheek against Adam's even as he spoke over the telephone. His arm slipped to her waist and he gave her a quick appraising glance.

The telephone conversation over, Adam put down the receiver and turned to look round for Francesca. He saw her on the stairs and called, 'Francesca, please, some coffee for Celia. She looks so cold.' Then he was talking swiftly and in a lowered voice and drawing Celia to the dining-room.

Francesca went back to the kitchen where she quickly laid a tray. Then she was surprised to see Celia herself looking in the doorway. She stared at her in astonishment.

'Coffee for Adam too, Miss Lamb,' Celia said, and there was a strange, sly little smile about her mouth. 'He'll have it with his brandy.' She pressed her lips together and then added, 'Please, don't keep us waiting.'

Swallowing her resentment, Francesca quickly made the coffee and took it to the dining-room. The moment she entered she knew at once that something was wrong. Celia was standing stiffly, her face pale with rage, her eyes hard on Adam, disbelieving. 'Giles coming home? I don't believe it. He can't be. He's ill. You know that, Adam.' Ignoring Francesca, she swung away to the window, her face convulsed with rage, as she said again, 'I don't believe it.'

'There's nothing mentally wrong, Celia, 'Adam went on in a controlled voice, gesturing to Francesca to put down the tray and leave them. 'He needs drugs, that's all. Sinclair knows what he's about. Giles doesn't need to be kept under supervision. He can return to Thorneyburn House whenever he likes.'

'But Adam, you know what he did?' Celia sounded distraught. 'How can he be sane?'

'Darling, you know what a practical joker he is. This time he carried things a bit too far, that's all. There's nothing seriously wrong with him.'

Francesca hurried to the door, but she heard Celia's voice rise shrilly as she told Adam, 'I still intend to be at your concert, Adam. Darling, I've got the most wonderful gown. You're going to be proud of me. Besides, Adam, I have some news for you, when Miss Lamb kindly closes the door.'

Back in the kitchen, Francesca went from job to job. She was trembling. Surely Adam would not weaken at such a time. Surely he would not take Celia away when Giles would need her so much. But what was it Celia had to tell him? Was it something that would make him change his mind at once? If it did, then she must alienate herself from such a man for ever. But how was she going to hate this man who made her ache so sweetly? How? she wondered with a fresh rush of panic. She would certainly struggle to fight against this insanity, this mockery of her good sense and reason. And if there was anything she could do to help Giles, anything at all she could do to ease the humiliation he must suffer, then she would be prepared to forget the past. She would be his friend, encourage him in moments of depression, try to help him to fight back. For Adam Greco was a strong adversary; talented, famous, handsome, rich. Poor Giles, he was not in a strong position. Like herself he would be tormented by uncer-

tainty. Tormented by indecision. Tormented by the
fact that without his money he had little to commend
him to a woman like Celia.

In her dreams that night, Francesca stirred little. She
smiled, smiled at the young man who had stopped his
car and offered to give both her mother and herself a
lift back to Thorneyburn Cottage. She thought how
nice he looked. She liked the way in which he smiled
at her. He made her laugh.

Then she was no longer laughing. She awoke with
a start. It was barely light, but at once Francesca knew
that someone was in her room. Holding her breath, she
raised herself a little. Then she dropped back again
with shock. Adam was standing over her, his hand
pressed to his mouth in a silencing gesture. Wide-eyed
with shock, she stared up at him. Was something
wrong? He was dressed in his outdoor clothes, his fur
collared coat, his fur hat.

'Francesca,' he whispered, and lowered himself
gently on to the side of her bed. 'I must go now, without Celia. Giles should be back at Thorneyburn House
this week, so you may not have her here long. But you
will look after her? Promise me that. Don't upset her.'

Francesca swallowed her resentment and sat up a
little. 'Why should I upset her?' she whispered back,
her eyes hard. 'And if I did, what difference would it
make? I'm sure Mrs Sutherland wouldn't waste a moment worrying about me.'

'Francesca, you don't understand. I'm afraid there's
no time for explanations. I only know that I'm in a
peculiar position and I'm asking you for your help.'
He took a deep breath and said under it, 'I know where
your sympathy lies and I'm sorry. But there it is.'

'Don't worry,' Francesca said reluctantly and with

just a hint of sarcasm, 'I'll look after Mrs Sutherland. Of course, should Giles come looking for his wife, then she'll be off my hands.'

Adam laughed softly. 'Good girl,' he said as he stood looking down at her with thoughtful eyes. 'And now wish me luck. I must go now.'

Francesca's expression changed. 'Of course I wish you luck, Adam,' she whispered, her heart suddenly full. 'Oh, I do wish you all the luck in the world, Adam. You know that.'

'Yes, I do, Francesca,' he said, still studying her earnestly. Then his eyes were glowing warmly and he stooped a little to draw the bedclothes gently over her shoulder. 'And we're going to have a wonderful Christmas, Francesca. We're going to bring this old house to life. We're both going to have a holiday, enjoy ourselves.'

Francesca raised herself a little. Once again she was aware of a great vacuum within herself, a vacuum aching to be filled. 'Adam,' she breathed, 'I know how you feel about Mrs Sutherland, but I'm glad you're going to London alone. Whatever you think of Giles he's going to need his wife at a time like this.'

Frowningly now, assessingly, Adam stood staring down at her. Then for some reason he sighed very deeply. 'I can't think why, Francesca,' he said in a strangely level tone, 'but the name Giles slips so easily from your tongue, never Mr Sutherland.' He smiled again. 'I do sometimes wonder,' he told her, then pausing and gesturing to match his words, he said more brusquely and glancing at his watch, 'but this is no time for conjecture or reflection. I really must go, Francesca.'

'Goodbye, Adam.' Francesca's smile was suddenly shy. 'Don't worry about anything here. Just please your public. Leave everything else to me. And good luck again.'

'Will you be thinking of me?'

Something in his eyes made Francesca catch her breath. She nodded.

'Goodbye, Francesca,' he whispered, and leaning forward he kissed her lightly upon her brow. 'Goodbye, my little housekeeper.'

Francesca shut her eyes tightly. She was trembling and he must not know it. She was willing herself not to reach up and draw him down. She was full of a powerful, thundering feeling of abandon. She no longer cared about anyone but herself and her feminine need of him, but he must not know it. She closed her eyes even more tightly as the blood thundered through her ears. For a terrifying moment she thought she would cry out; the agony of wanting him was so terrible. Then she held her breath, for now she felt the firm pressure of his hand running over her shoulder and back, a pressure which translated itself into an agonisingly sweet ache wherever the caressingly firm palm moved. Suddenly she turned on to her back. Aroused now, she stared up at him; she could not speak, she could not smile.

But Adam smiled down at her as he gently tipped up her chin and kissed her quickly. 'I must go,' he said brusquely again. 'Goodbye, Francesca.'

Francesca did not move until she heard his car moving over the gravel drive, then she sat up very slowly, like someone coming out of a deep dream. It was dawn; the great apricot sun was just rising from a misty horizon. Francesca got up and tiptoed to the window. Down over the fields she could just see the roof of Thorneyburn Cottage caught now in a web of gold.

Suddenly she felt happier than she had done for a while. She danced back to the bedside. Yes, she told herself, she felt happy. Adam had gone without Celia! Her wonderful dark-eyed genius had a conscience after all. Celia Sutherland could not destroy him. Seduce him, she might well, but what was that? Celia could never get to the heart of the man. Suddenly Francesca was laughing softly—and at herself. She was the one with no heart. She was going downstairs to break the news to Mrs Sutherland. She could not stop smiling.

After washing and making up her face a little, she pulled on her jeans and a warm roll-necked sweater. She hurried downstairs, pausing for a few moments to gaze fondly at her old clock. Then she glanced at the sturdy banister rails and remembered with a pang how she had once helped her mother to decorate them with holly and fir one Christmas. This Christmas she would do the same, she decided with a fresh rush of excitement. Old Beams would look wonderful. She would make a real Christmas for Adam, one he would never forget. She would start making plans at once. She knew the Nobles would do their utmost to help. Perhaps she would invite them into the house for a special Christmas meal. Adam would play for them; give them a special thrill. Yes, it was to be a wonderful Christmas.

Lowering her eyelids, Francesca steadied herself. Adam was fond of her. Yes, that was undoubtedly so. And he needed her, that was also true. Yet—Francesca's expression changed as different thoughts came galloping savagely into her mind. She spun round quickly and hurried to the kitchen, her face very straight again. her new confidence waning. Here she was foolishly making plans, changing the course of her life, and all because Adam Greco had kissed her lightly and run a firm, encouraging hand over her back. Her lips pulled contemptuously. Probably he had imagined she was cold, that was all. He had still left her the unpleasant task of telling Mrs Sutherland that he had gone off to London without her.

At nine o'clock Francesca put aside the list she had been making and wandered out into the hall. Frowning a little, she wondered if she should call Celia, then just as she decided against doing so, she heard a movement on the landing and Celia appeared on the staircase wrapped in a warm yet still seductive-looking woollen robe.

'I was just about to call you, Mrs Sutherland,' Francesca said as Celia reached the hall. 'Are you all right?'

'Of course I'm all right.' Celia Sutherland yawned and then scowled. 'Why shouldn't I be? Do I look ill?'

'No, of course not.' Francesca took a deep breath. 'It's just that I know Mr Greco usually calls you.'

'Yes, he does.' Celia looked away towards the sitting room. 'Where is he? Has he had breakfast? I could do with some coffee.'

'Mr Greco left early,' Francesca returned directly. 'He's off to London. He didn't want to disturb you, so he left me to break the news.'

'London?' Celia Sutherland jerked up as though stung by a wasp. 'What do you mean?' she asked coldly, her eyes upon Francesca unflinching. 'Is this some kind of a joke?'

'Not that I know of,' Francesca said lightly as she moved away in the direction of the kitchen. 'Mr Greco has rehearsals all week. This must be an anxious time for him.' She glanced back. 'He asked me to let you know that he would be in touch.'

'Really?' Celia's throat worked and her eyes were

hard and bright. 'How kind of you, Miss Lamb.' For a moment she pursed her lips in a sarcastic gesture, then she threw back her head and laughed. 'How utterly ridiculous that man can be at times,' she said bitingly. 'Of course, I must follow him. These talented men can be so impulsive. I'll have that coffee now, Miss Lamb, then you must help me to pack. I must go right after him. He'll expect it, so don't stand there gaping. Believe me, I know Adam Greco. I know his every whim.' She walked ahead of Francesca now, calling as she went into the dining room, 'Don't imagine for one moment that your news has upset me.'

Francesca stood perfectly still, then on a deep breath she said levelly, 'In my opinion Mr Greco needs some time alone, Mrs Sutherland. He hasn't been getting down to his work lately and there's only a week before his concert.'

Celia turned slowly. For a moment she moistened her lips, then with deliberate intensity she said, 'So you're really hoping to keep me here, Miss Lamb. You're jealous, aren't you?' Her lips curled contemptuously, then she laughed again. 'If I didn't know so much about you, Miss Lamb, I'd have credited you with an amazing imagination. But then I do, thanks to my housekeeper, Mrs Coates, who now remembers you quite well. You're not exactly a newcomer to Old Beams, are you, Miss Lamb?'

Francesca turned deathly white. She opened her mouth to speak, but Celia raised her hand and went on viciously, 'Yes, I know your little game, Miss Lamb. I know why you came back here. You came back for Giles, didn't you? Perhaps you'd even heard that he wasn't getting on too well with his rich wife? And then Adam was kind. You little fool, you may even be imagining that he prefers to be without me. Well, I have news for you, Miss Lamb. I'm going straight off to London now because I happen to have news for Adam. News which may interest you.' A triumphant light in her eyes now, Celia straightened up to her full height. 'Great news,' she went on excitedly, her voice growing shrill, 'news which will certainly bring you to your senses, Miss Lamb. Wonderful news for Adam. You see,' she went on, smiling now, 'I saw a gynaecologist yesterday, Miss Lamb. He confirmed my suspicion. I'm pregnant. I'm to have a child.'

It was a deafening emotion that rose from within Francesca, spreading through her veins and bringing with it a feeling of sickness and nausea. Despairingly she stared back into Celia's enormous and feverishly bright eyes. A strangled moan struggled in her throat and died. She could not speak, she felt as though she had withered and grown old in moments. Slowly she turned away, for she could not look at Celia Sutherland any longer. She only knew that she felt dead within. The house too seemed like a tomb now, deathly cold and still.

There was a sound of the door shutting and, looking round, Francesca saw that Celia had gone from the room. For a few more moments she stood very still, then, fighting to pull herself together, she made her way back to the kitchen. So Adam Greco's light kiss and firm caress had been no more than a bribe, she thought as she gazed through blurred eyes out of the window. All the time he had known about Celia's condition. No wonder he had been concerned! As for Mrs Coates having recognized her, that mattered not a jot now. And Giles! Poor, poor weak Giles. Suddenly Francesca covered her face with her hands. She could not stay to see him so humiliated, finally brought down. Somehow she had to struggle free, struggle with all her strength to get away from the ghastly web of intrigue in which she had been caught. She had to say her last farewell to Northumberland. For loving Adam Greco as she did, she could never return. She would go on loving him, she would not be able to help herself. But she no longer believed in miracles. She knew now that she could never return to the small cottage down over the fields where she had once been so happy. It was time to stop dreaming.

CHAPTER EIGHT

STILL trembling from shock, Francesca shakily made herself a pot of tea. What could she do? What ought she to do? Leave without a word? That was just what she had done with her last job, she reminded herself with some chagrin. There was a bus back to town at two o'clock. She could be at the crossroads by then. She stirred some sugar vigorously into her tea. The tea slopped over on to the saucer and through angry tears she stared disgustedly at it. Then she drank what was left and immediately felt better. Why was she so dismayed? she asked herself critically. She had known for long enough about the relationship between Celia Sutherland and Adam. Why was she so overcome? Why did she feel so weak, so shocked? Again a fresh gust of horror swept over her. She had to go. How could she possibly stay? How could she be fool enough to go on loving Adam Greco?

Fresh air was what she needed, she decided, to cool and calm her brain. She had to get out of the house and breathe in the sweet, moorland air. The breeze that swept down from the hills and stirred the grass would have all the answers. For a moment, her hatred of Celia Sutherland died down. She went out into the silent hall, picked up her jacket and glanced back at the half open dining-room door. There was no sound, no movement. Had Celia gone? Frowning, Francesca tiptoed to the doorway and peered in.

From the fireplace Celia smiled coolly back at Francesca and at once all the hatred was back in Francesca's heart. 'There's some tea in the pot,' she said flatly. 'I'm going out.' And because of the arrogant mockery in Celia's eyes she said defiantly, 'And as I don't happen to be in your employ, Mrs Sutherland, I have no intention of packing your case.'

Celia looked cool. 'Don't imagine for one moment that you ever will be in my employ, Miss Lamb,' she said levelly. 'I think we will very soon be able to dispense with your services.'

Rage thundered in Francesca's ears. For a few moments she glared silently at Celia, then she turned and swiftly made her way out of the house. That settled everything, she thought as another wave of fury made her reel. She would catch the two o'clock bus back to town. But first of all she would see Mrs Noble. She must at least say farewell to her friends and leave instructions for the rest of the week. She would need a reference, after all, and even now she did not want Adam to think badly of her.

'Hello? Is there something wrong?' Mrs Noble's eyes widened the moment she opened her door and saw Francesca standing there, looking deeply troubled. 'Come in,' she went on quickly. 'There's something wrong; I can see by your face. Mrs Sutherland's on her high horse. I knew she'd start the moment Mr Greco got away.' Leading Francesca into her kitchen and pulling up a chair for her, she urged her to sit down as she went on, 'Come on, get it off your chest. Then we'll have a nice cup of tea. Now calm down, lassie. There's no need for you to get into such a state over her. Although, God knows, Thomas swears that one would lead her own grandfather astray if there was money in it. He can't abide the sight of Mrs Sutherland.'

'She's going,' Francesca said, her eyes lowered. 'She's following Mr Greco to London. There's really no need for me to stay.'

'Chasing him to London now, is she?' Mrs Noble's voice rang with contempt. 'And her with a husband so sick. Poor man, no wonder he's had a breakdown. That woman would break any man. She could swallow a serpent, she's that hard. Destroy the strongest. Down in the village they tell me Giles Sutherland used to be such a nice, kindly young man. Of course the whole family had the Midas touch. His parents got it into him very young that anything he touched must turn to gold. That's why he married Celia Sutherland, so they tell me.'

Francesca took the fresh cup of tea Mrs Noble quickly poured out for her. She found the woman's motherly tone encouraging and soon she found herself smiling as Mrs Noble rattled on confidently, 'I hope you weren't thinking of running away. You'll have to make a stand —at least until Mr Greco gets back. It's all part of your training, lass.'

'Perhaps I am being rather silly,' Francesca confessed at last, determined though not to give Mrs Noble the full facts lest the glad tidings were around the village before even Adam heard them. She averted her head as these cynical thoughts twisted her mouth and dulled her eyes. 'It must be one of my off days,' she went on with a forced laugh. 'Mrs Sutherland was rather off-hand and I'm afraid I was very rude. I'm sorry I've put you to all this trouble, Mrs Noble. Thank you you for being so understanding.'

'Drop in any time, lass. We love to see you.' Mrs

Noble smiled rather knowingly at Francesca's bowed head. 'And don't you worry about Mr Greco. He's a strong man. Somehow I can't see Mrs Sutherland making a fool of him. He's too keen on his music. He's not going to give everything up to see the headline, Famous composer seduces sick man's wife.'

'I wouldn't know,' Francesca said breathlessly, standing up and turning to the door. 'In any case, it's really no business of mine.'

'You're staying, then?'

Francesca looked back. 'Oh yes,' she said over a lump in her throat. 'I'm staying, Mrs Noble. I've made up my mind to make you and Mr Noble a Christmas dinner you're not likely to forget. We'll have a good time.'

'Good girl! We'll look forward to it.' Mrs Noble escorted Francesca to the door. 'And you can rely on me to do some special cleaning. We'll really brighten the whole place up.'

With a grateful smile, Francesca hurried away. Then the sound of a car made her draw up. The car turned and skidded past her. She watched it go, then hurriedly made her way back into the big house. Celia had lost no time. She had gone. At the speed she drove, she would very soon be in London. Very soon now, Celia and Adam would be together discussing their plans for the future, plans which would undoubtedly exclude both herself and Giles.

Pensively, Francesca stared out of the window, her gaze rising from the rank grass of the garden to the tall pines and then up to the black mass of rock above. Winter would soon come now, she thought, and with it the snow, but then would come spring and with the slow thaw perhaps her own anguish would melt away. Mrs Noble was right, she must stay. She admitted that she had a strong desire to be at Old Beams at Christmas. She had promised herself a walk over the fields to Thorneyburn Cottage on Christmas Day. She wanted to look in the windows of her old home, she wanted so much to revive old memories, bring back feelings she had thought forgotten. She had once been so happy, so safe there.

Yet she had no intention of staying at Old Beams for long. After New Year, she would make new plans.

Later, after a quick tidy about the house, Francesca returned to the kitchen. It was a bright morning now, the sun's rays streamed encouragingly through the window and the sky above the black rock was like a strip of blue silk. It was the day to make the Christmas cake, she decided, and she quickly began to arrange her cooking equipment. As she worked she thought about Adam and his new concerto, the Golden Concerto for which he had told her that she herself had been the inspiration.

The telephone rang shrilly, jerking Francesca out of her thoughts and sending her rushing to the hall. Was it Adam?

It was the hospital. Francesca drew her breath in alarm. It was Mr Sinclair and he wanted to speak to Mrs Sutherland, who he understood was staying at Old Beams.

'I'm afraid Mrs Sutherland isn't in,' Francesca answered carefully. 'This is Miss Lamb, Mr Greco's housekeeper, speaking.'

'And Mr Greco?'

'Mr Greco is in London for one of his concerts.'

'I see.' There was a pause, then the voice went on brusquely, 'Then you must give me the hotel telephone number. This is important, Miss Lamb. Mr Sutherland has discharged himself from my care and he is now on his way home to Thorneyburn House.'

There was another pause and then the deep masculine voice went on. 'You can give Mrs Sutherland this message when she comes in. Tell her there's nothing to worry about. Mr Sutherland should be perfectly all right if he takes things easy and keeps calm. He has a supply of tablets with him. You could ask Mrs Sutherland to get in touch with me here at the hospital.'

'Yes ... yes, I'll do that.' Francesca felt a rush of blood to her head. 'Yes, I'll tell her. Thank you, Mr Sinclair. Good morning.'

With a shaking hand she put down the receiver. Giles coming home! Wasn't it just like him to discharge himself? How would he keep calm when he found that his wife wasn't even at home or at Old Beams, that she was far away in London with Adam? Panicking, Francesca ran to the sitting room where she frantically searched among the papers on Adam's desk. She had to telephone Adam at once. Celia would have to return—she must. She would put it to Adam Greco in no uncertain terms. She picked up a letter and read the heading, then she ran back to the hall with it. Adam would be at his hotel now. It was almost one o'clock. Excited, frightened, she picked up the receiver and waited to be put through to him. Her heart beat fast, her legs felt weak.

'Yes? Adam Greco here.'

Francesca took a deep breath. 'Adam!' she gasped. 'This is Francesca. I had to ring.' She took another deep breath. 'Mr Sinclair has just telephoned to say that Giles has left hospital of his own accord. He's on his way home. He said he must keep calm and take his drugs.'

'What's wrong with that?' There was no hesitation on Adam Greco's part. 'That's splendid news, Francesca. And thank you for ringing. I've just got in.'

'But, Adam——'

'Has Celia gone home?' he cut in, his voice more sober.

'Adam,' Francesca gulped, 'Celia is on her way to London. She's determined to be with you.' Her voice lost some of its strength as she went on, 'And you know why.'

'God in heaven!' Adam's voice changed again. 'Didn't you give her my message?' Decidedly angry now, he raged on, 'I thought you understood, Francesca. I can't have her here. I don't want her here at the moment.'

Another pause. Francesca felt herself turning white. 'Mr Greco,' she began again, bracing herself and clipping each word decisively, 'being a famous man doesn't entitle you to have your own way all the time. To steal may be easy, but to keep hidden what you've stolen may now prove much more difficult.'

'What the devil are you talking about, Francesca?'

Another silence prolonged itself miserably.

'Will you send Celia back?' Francesca broke in at last. 'She does happen to be Giles's wife.'

'Of course I'll send her back. I'll send her packing the moment she arrives. I thought you understood. I must work this week, Francesca, I need the time. You know that.'

'I know everything, Adam.'

'Are you tired, Francesca? Or ill?' His voice rang back sharply.

'I'm perfectly all right.'

'Then carry on. Leave this to me. But one word of

warning—if Giles is at home, don't go over there. And, Francesca, don't forget to lock up each night. I'm worried about you.'

'Shouldn't you be worried about Celia?' Francesca's voice was cold and flat.

'Of course I'm worried. I'm damn well worried about everyone!' Adam's voice rang with impatience. 'Promise me you'll lock up. And don't venture across to Thorneyburn House at least until I get back.'

'You think Giles is still ill, then?'

'I'd prefer not to say what I think at the moment, Francesca. Leave everything to me. Just carry on as usual until I get back. And wish me luck.' His voice lowered. 'You could do that.'

'Oh, yes, Adam,' she whispered. 'I do wish you luck with your concert. I do.'

'Thank you, Francesca. I'll be in touch. Goodbye for the time being.'

Francesca put down the receiver and for a few moments she stood still, conscious only of the throbbing in her brain. The very sound of Adam's voice seemed to inflame her mind. He attacked her like an illness; the thought of him even now destroyed the last vestiges of her common sense. She should have been more direct, more critical. She thought of him with a mixture of rage and desire. She both pitied and hated herself for her weakness. In the throes of despair, she wondered what would become of, not Adam Greco the lover, but Adam Greco the musician. Would Celia have the power to destroy this brilliant man? It was strange that in a permissive age the world still rejected such behaviour. And Giles! Poor Giles! What would he do when he returned to his home and found it empty? Another thought flashed through her head and pulled her up.

She caught her breath and again indignation and anger came to her aid. Adam was in no position to tell her what she must do or not do. If Giles did ring, she would tell him the truth, that Celia was on her way home. If he came to Old Beams she would be kind. She was not afraid of him—there was no reason for her to be—just sorry.

With a feeling of unease Francesca set about her work again. Once the cake was safely in the oven she helped Mrs Noble to put up new curtains and change some of the soiled cushion covers in preparation for Christmas. After tea Thomas Noble came in and went up into the attics to get the hampers down. He was as excited as a small boy. He was in high spirits because he had been asked to help decorate the village church.

'You've both been a wonderful help to me,' Francesca confessed to Mrs Noble once her husband had gone off again. 'I expect you thought I was a bit ridiculous at first.' She laughed a little. 'All that business about calling me Miss Lamb.'

Mrs Noble laughed affectionately. 'You were just inexperienced,' she went on goodnaturedly. 'Thomas and I had to smile. You looked so valiant. We knew you weren't old enough to have had any experience. But I must say you managed astonishingly well. The old place seemed to take you, just as we did. You seemed to fit in.' Mrs Noble frowned thoughtfully. 'It's strange, isn't it, how you can feel these things. Now when Mrs Sutherland appears you can hear this place's old bones creak.'

'She should be back at Thorneyburn House tonight,' Francesca told Mrs Noble. 'Mr Sutherland came home today. I had to ring Mr Greco and tell him.' She lowered her eyes and went on, 'I only hope it won't be too late for her to get back.'

'I suppose Mr Greco will have all the trouble of driving Mrs Sutherland back,' Mrs Noble pronounced with a sigh of disgust.

Francesca looked up. 'Oh, I shouldn't think so,' she said hesitantly. 'Mr Greco has rehearsals all week. I expect Mrs Sutherland will drive tomorrow.'

'I hope so,' Mrs Noble rushed on, her brow creasing with exasperation. 'Even if the doctor does say he's all right, Mr Sutherland shouldn't be left alone. They're too fond of pushing everyone on to pills these days.'

'I must look at the cake,' Francesca said swiftly, fighting to drive from her mind the fact that Celia would make the most of the one night she had to spend with Adam. 'I think we've worked hard enough for one day, Mrs Noble. You can go, I'll clear up.'

Mrs Noble's lips tightened as though to imprison the words that were already on her tongue. But her gaze followed Francesca until at last with a sigh she turned to the door. 'Will you come across later?' she asked, glancing back. 'There's a good programme on television tonight.'

Francesca shook her head. 'Thanks,' she said, 'but there are one or two things I must do. And I think I'll have an early night. Tomorrow we'll have a busy day emptying all the hampers Mr Noble brought down.'

'We'll enjoy that,' Mrs Noble said as she opened the door. 'Thomas always gets excited about Christmas.' She paused and stared frowningly at Francesca for a moment, then went on in a motherly tone, 'And don't you worry about anyone but yourself, Francesca. Believe me, girl, there'll always be somebody else.'

Francesca swallowed hard as Mrs Noble closed the door behind her and when she finally went upstairs to her bedroom at ten o'clock she was still pondering over her words of wisdom. But they were untrue, she told herself as she stared back into her mirror. There would be no one else for her. She would go on loving Adam Greco for ever and ever. Foolishly, she would go on loving a man who had already given his greatest gift of love to another woman. If Celia divorced Giles and married Adam, then she might even offer her services to Giles. He would need a housekeeper.

As she stood before her mirror wild thoughts trampled through Francesca's weary head. Finally she fell into bed, but it was hours before she at last grew calm and fell into a merciful sleep.

She woke with a start. The room was in darkness, the house was silent and yet fear crept up her spine. Instinct told her that there was danger in the darkness, that she was not alone in the house. Above the frightening clamour of her heart she strained to hear the least sound. Still listening, she slowly sat up. Then she went stiff with fear ...

A fine stream of light had suddenly appeared beneath the bedroom door. Someone had switched on a light. There was someone else in the house—and they were coming upstairs! Was it Adam? For a moment she prayed that such miracles still occurred. She even called out brokenly, 'Adam, is that you?' She nibbled her thumbnail and then another thought flashed through her mind. It was Mrs Noble. She had left something and come back for it. Francesca glanced at her bedside clock. At two o'clock in the morning? No, it was not Mrs Noble. A burglar! Why had she foolishly left the front door unlocked? The idea of a burglar brought an angry flush to her face. She pushed back the bedclothes.

Then the light snapped on. The harsh glare brought

her hands to her eyes, but she had seen who stood in the doorway. 'Giles?' she gasped. 'Giles, whatever are you doing here?' She turned to reach for her robe, suddenly conscious of her naked shoulders. She was trembling, her heart racing, and very aware of the insolent look in Giles's cold eyes. 'I'll come down,' she said, fighting to keep her voice firm.

'Stay where you are.' He laughed oddly, with a hint of hysteria.

Francesca met his gaze. As he approached her bed she saw how deathly pale he was, how the purple shadows were accentuated beneath his eyes. His expression was shifty, uncertain. 'Giles,' she said firmly and with slow deliberation, 'you are not in a position to walk into my bedroom. At this hour it's unforgivable. You gave me a terrible shock. I thought the house was being burgled.'

His gaze was intent as he stood by the side of the bed gazing down at her. 'But you left the door open nevertheless. You knew I was coming, Francesca. After all, I'm not sick now and I couldn't have asked you to come over to Thorneyburn House...'

Francesca sat forward clutching the bedclothes, her eyes flickering with fear. 'Celia will be back tomorrow,' she told him falteringly. 'She went to London for the concert, but now that she knows you're home, she's coming back, Giles. Everything is going to be all right.'

'Yes,' Giles reiterated, 'everything is going to be all right, Francesca, because I'm going to make it so. You came back to Old Beams to find me and now I've come to Old Beams to find you. You belong to me, Francesca, you always did. You're mine and I've come to claim you, to set my seal upon you. I'm no longer afraid, Francesca. No longer afraid to take what's mine.'

179

Francesca took a deep breath. She was shaking violently, but she managed to say, 'Let me get you a drink, Giles. Let's go downstairs. It's late, but it doesn't really matter.'

'It doesn't matter at all, Francesca. We're alone. Celia, my wife, and Adam are far enough away. We have all the time in the world. But we're not going downstairs.'

In one swift glance Francesca saw the savage which lurks closely beneath all civilized veneer. Too frightened to move now, she bowed her head.

'Oh, how I've loved you, Francesca, dreamt of you, wanted you ...'

Giles's voice rose to an anguished moan and Francesca knew that she must do something at once. He was still ill—she could see it in his eyes. And she no longer pitied him. 'You're sick, sick! And I don't want you, Giles. I don't love you ...' She flung back the bedclothes and made an attempt to get out of bed. Frantically she shruggled with him.

'But you do, Francesca.'

Helplessly, she stared back at him as steely fingers turned about her wrist, as she was pressed back upon the bed. The intensity of his gaze made her blood run cold. In the depths of his eyes she saw the long-suppressed torment, the agony and the frenzy which gripped him. 'Giles,' she begged. 'Giles, no ... No!'

But Giles had been thwarted too long and for him there was no turning back. Aggressively now, he pressed Francesca back and down, deeper down, and like a snake he slid on to the bed and coiled about her. His low laugh seemed to curdle in his throat.

Then Francesca felt the harshness of his breath against her face, his desperate body against her own.

She shut her eyes tightly, turned her face, her mouth away from his.

'Francesca, I'm not going to hurt you.'

'You are hurting me!'

'I must prove to you that you still want me as much as ever. I know you do.'

His lips moved roughly across her averted face, found and imprisoned her trembling lips. 'There,' he gasped after a few moments, 'there, you see, you do care.' He drew up and stared down into her wide, terrified eyes. 'You still want me.' His voice rose excitedly and with some hysteria. 'I can see it in your eyes, Francesca, in your soft skin, in your hair.' Charged with desire, he cried out, 'I love you, Francesca. You know I'm crazy about you. I've always been crazy about you.'

Suddenly Francesca found the strength to fight back against Giles's desperate attempt to make her love him. 'You're disgusting!' she shouted, but this time her voice broke. Her mind seemed to stop functioning and she just lay kicking and struggling against a determined body which fought for predominance over her own, against hands which sent a loathing and hatred over her whole skin ... against lips ...

A great beam of light spread over the bedroom walls and she cried out again, and this time strongly, triumphantly. 'It's Adam! It's Adam!' she called. 'Look, Giles, there's a car coming up the drive. Adam's home! He's come back.'

Again the headlights of a car beamed across the room and again Giles ignored them. Francesca saw only the expression of dangerous and stubborn intent upon his rapt face, the expression of a man who meant to get his own way whatever happened. Gathering her strength, she struggled up again. 'Look, Giles!' she shouted as loud as she possibly could. 'Look at the headlights! It's Adam. He's back!'

This time Giles started up and for a moment his grip upon her loosened. With another cry, Francesca leapt from the bed and ran sobbing from the room. Staggering, calling 'Adam! Adam!' she made her way along the landing to the stairhead. She gripped the banister rail with trembling fingers. But she was unable to take another step; she felt too weak, too shocked, too afraid that the lights which had beamed across the room had belonged not to Adam's but to some other passing car.

The front door burst open and the hall below was suddenly flooded with light. Francesca stood like a ghost. She wanted to cry out, but no sound would come from her violated throat. She wanted to move, to run down the stairs, but her outraged limbs would not move. Was she seeing things? she asked herself. Was it really Adam Greco who stood there staring up at her, his eyes so full of concern? Adam Greco, so dark, so handsome?

Below, in the hall, Adam caught his breath at the sight of the bowed figure at the top of the stairs. 'My God!' he muttered, and in a moment he was leaping up the staircase. 'My God!' he cried out again as he reached out and took her into his arms. He searched her ashen face, her blank eyes. 'Francesca!' he suddenly called in a desperate voice. 'Francesca! It's me—Adam! Everything is going to be all right.' And gathering her close again, 'Oh, Francesca!'

Hysterical now, Francesca beat her small fists upon his chest. Hysterically she cried, 'You did this to him! You did this to poor Giles! You took his wife away, his pride.'

Adam's dark face worked with emotion. His grip on her arm grew steely, painful. 'Calm yourself,' he said in a voice as firm as his grip, and as his gaze fell upon the flushed, aggravated skin of her shoulders, his whole body set and tensed with rage. His throat worked as he looked away over her head. 'Giles is here, isn't he?' he said harshly. 'He's in your room.'

He stood away from her a little, his eyes still riveted upon her face, eyes full of stupefaction now, disbelief. Then, still without a word, he turned and strode away. Francesca watched him push open the bedroom door and then stand perfectly still again, his lips pursed tightly in contempt and impatience. Then he laughed. 'The sleep of the just ... I hope,' he called back to Francesca. 'Just come and gaze on your lover now.' And striding back to her he stood glaring down at her for a few moments before he said coldly, 'So I'm the one who's given you a shock, unnerved you. I disturbed the great lovers, did I? Is that it? I am an intruder in my own house?' He flung back his dark, magnificent head contemptuously. 'So what Celia had to tell me was true. You actually came back to Old Beams with the intention of pestering someone else's husband.' Stooping a little, he glared even more fiercely into the white mask which was Francesca's face.

'Adam!' Francesca caught his hand and clung to it. 'Adam, listen to me. Giles has only been here ten minutes. I woke up and found him in the house. I struggled with him ... I fought ... Then I saw the headlights of your car.' Weak with shock she whimpered, 'I was so thankful. Oh, Adam, don't say such things!' Again her pride restored her. She took a deep breath, braved his eyes again. 'Besides,' she rushed on before her nerve broke again, 'what right have you to upbraid me, Mr Greco? I wouldn't call you a moral man. I suppose Celia did give you the rest of the news. She did tell you that she was pregnant, that you would very soon be a father?'

Now she could not look at him. She stood with bowed head as time ticked away. The cards were on the table now; there was no going back.

'Francesca,' she heard him say levelly and from what seemed like a thousand miles away, 'I'm very pleased about the baby. Celia's news delights me. But I must disappoint you. I do not happen to be the father. Giles is.'

'Giles?' At last Francesca raised pained eyes. 'Giles?' she breathed. 'But you told me ...'

Adam shrugged his shoulders. 'Doctors can be wrong. Giles's handicap was obviously a temporary one. Don't you think you've been rather hasty in your conclusion, Francesca? I'm not condemning you. I'm sorry ... disappointed ...'

'Adam! Adam, please let me explain.' Francesca felt her knees sag again. Tears blurred her vision. She wanted to throw herself against him and tell him all she had suffered, all the wrong things she had imagined about him. But her head was reeling again and she felt dizzy. 'Why won't you ...?'

Her voice faded as she sank to the floor. She did not hear Adam cry out, nor did she feel the strong arms that picked her up and carried her downstairs. But two minutes later she felt the cold water that trickled down from her lips and opening her eyes she saw Adam standing over her and knew at once that she had fainted. She said nothing, and he sat down beside her on the settee before the fire. 'I'm all right,' she whispered. 'And I'll be quite well enough to leave Old

184

Beams in the morning.' For a moment she raised her eyes to his. 'It seems that I owe you an apology,' she breathed, then she turned quickly away from him again.

'Just close your eyes,' he told her. 'Don't worry about a thing, Francesca. It seems we all make mistakes.' He took her hand between in his own in a comforting gesture.

For a few minutes they sat very still and in silence, then Adam stood up and after reaching for a rug he pressed it firmly about Francesca's shoulders. 'I'll stir up the fire,' he said, and turned to the hearth. 'Who knows, we may even see a brighter future in its flames.' He threw on a few logs, and then asked, 'Do you feel better now, Francesca?'

Francesca shook her head. 'I'll feel better when you know the truth,' she said stubbornly and beginning to shiver again. 'Or will you never believe me?'

He stared down at her for a moment. 'Don't get upset again,' he said in a firm voice. 'Does it matter what I believe?'

'You believe Celia.'

He frowned and shrugged his shoulders. 'Not always,' he said, and a slow smile curved his lips. 'Remember, I've known Celia for many years. She's incredibly vain, an utter snob and fearfully selfish, but she's not a tramp, Francesca. I couldn't have her maligned in that direction.' He suddenly laughed out abruptly. 'But of course I can't say I didn't find her very desirable.'

'I don't want to hear about it.' Francesca went hot and then cold again. She tried to struggle up, but fell weakly back again. 'But I do want you to know this, Adam,' she went on, and she raised her eyes to him beseechingly. 'It's true that I once lived here. I lived with my mother down at Thorneyburn Cottage. I loved the place. I loved my mother. I know now that I would have even married Giles Sutherland for my mother's sake. My mother worked here in this house and subconsciously I suppose I wished she'd been the mistress of the house instead of the housekeeper. And then, because of pressure by his parents, Giles turned me down and married Celia. My mother died and I crept away to London where I was even more unhappy. Then I read your advertisement and I just had to come home. I had to come back to Northumberland and relive old memories. You know how often I walked over to Thorneyburn Cottage. I went over to peer through those small windows and pretend that all was well again, that my mother was there, that she was waiting for me. I could see her. I could see myself. I deluded myself, Adam, and I was happy.'

Adam gave her a swift glance and then turned to the fire again. He stood with his feet slightly apart, his features set gravely as he stared down into the living flames. 'Go on,' he said. 'I'm doing my best to understand.'

'That's all, Adam. Except that I never dreamt of finding Giles here. I thought he was far away in New Zealand.'

'You were pleased to see him?' His head bowed a little more steeply. 'He was part of your dream?'

'No, Adam.' Francesca's voice rose hysterically again. 'I was shocked. Giles wanted to start all over again. He pleaded with me. Obviously he was an unhappy man. But I knew then that I'd never loved him. I was sorry for him, that's all. Sorry when I saw how he was being . . .'

'Deceived?' Adam swung round and his voice was

186

sharp, his eyes hard. 'You really were seeing things, Francesca Lamb. And reading far too much in an imaginary script.' He sighed, long and hard, then went on almost abruptly, 'If it hadn't been for the Sutherlands' money Celia could well have married me years ago. We happened to remain friends, that's all. I saw how things were going and I tried to help. It was madness, of course.'

'Do you still want her?' Francesca's voice was barely audible, yet it made him jerk to attention.

'Want her?' He laughed roughly. 'I suppose any man could want Celia. I join with you, Francesca, in wishing that Giles and Celia will be happy. I think they will be. This baby is going to make all the difference. It will make a woman of Celia and give poor Giles a boost. The very fact that he'll be a father will have a good effect upon his ego.'

'And you, Adam? You must go on with your music. You don't belong to yourself. You belong to the world.'

He studied her curiously for a few moments, her pale anxious face, her wide, upraised eyes. Then he muttered under his breath and in a moment he was on the settee beside Francesca, drawing her into his arms, crushing her close to his own warm, vibrating body. 'And what about us, Francesca?' he whispered huskily. 'What about you and me?' Again he held her back, searched her face. 'Will you ever forgive me? I did for one moment think the worst—that you hadn't attempted to turn poor Giles away.' He tensed up, his voice grew full of urgency. With a rush of passion he drew the rug down from Francesca's shoulders and buried his face against her soft skin. 'Couldn't you find it in your heart to pity me? God knows how much I need you, Francesca. I love you.' His dark, magnificent eyes drew closed for a moment. 'I don't want to belong to the world, Francesca, I want to belong to you. Didn't my music tell you so? Couldn't you hear what I had to say?'

Feverishly she stared back at him. 'Adam,' she cried as she clung to him. 'Oh, Adam, I love you. I never loved any man until I loved you.' Her eyes grew shy and her lips trembled as she drew back again. 'Tell me,' she breathed, 'tell me, Adam, why did you come back? Were you afraid for my life? Or my virtue?'

Again he held her tightly to his chest. 'When Celia told me about you and Giles I only knew one thing,' he told her passionately. 'I knew I had a rival. I knew too that I meant to fight back. I just bundled poor Celia into the car and drove and drove. I was desperate, Francesca, desperately afraid that what Celia said was true, that you still hankered after Giles. Then, when I got here and saw you standing up there on the landing ...'

'You thought the worst.' Francesca struggled free. 'Well,' she said, smiling, 'I forgive you.'

He looked at her for a long time, then he stood up, drawing Francesca at the same time to her feet. Then they were fast in each other's arms.

At last Francesca drew away from him, leaving only her hand in his. 'Let's go to the door,' she said in a wistful tone. 'I want to look at the stars, Adam. I'm so happy.'

He gave her a long, loving look, a look of infinite understanding. 'You want to look over the fields to Thorneyburn Cottage, don't you, Francesca?'

'Yes, I do, Adam. For the last time.' She smiled almost secretly and drew him away. 'There'll be no time for reliving memories now.'

Her face was grave as she opened the heavy oak door. Then they were smiling at each other ... laughing. For like a blessing, a shower of confetti, the first flurries of snow came rushing at them.

Francesca clung to Adam again, her arms about his neck, her eyes searching his. 'Adam,' she said, and her young voice broke with emotion, 'the gift of love is a wonderful thing.'

Send for your copy today!

The Harlequin Romance Catalog FREE!

Here's your chance to catch up on all the wonderful Harlequin Romance novels you may have missed because the books are no longer available at your favorite booksellers.

Complete the coupon and mail it to us. By return mail, we'll send you a copy of the latest Harlequin catalog. Then you'll be able to order the books you want directly from us.

Clip and mail coupon today.

Send for free catalog

Most of these old favorites have not been reissued since first publication. So if you read them then, you'll enjoy them again; if they're new to you, you'll have the pleasure of discovering a new series of compelling romances from past years.

Collection Editions are available only from Harlequin Reader Service. They are not sold in stores.

Clip and mail this special coupon. We will send you a catalog listing all the Collection Editions titles and authors.